Narcissa and Other Fables

Narcissa

AND OTHER FABLES

Louis Auchincloss

HOUGHTON MIFFLIN COMPANY
BOSTON
1983

Library of Congress Cataloging in Publication Data

Auchincloss, Louis.
Narcissa, and other fables.

Contents: Narcissa — The seagull — The ghost of
Hamlet's ghost — [etc.]
I. Title.
PS3501.U25N3   1983   813'.54   82-12086
ISBN 0-395-33114-5

Printed in the United States of America

s 10 9 8 7 6 5 4 3 2 1

"The Seagull" first appeared in the *Atlantic,* May 1979.
"The Ghost of Hamlet's Ghost" first appeared in
Harper's Bazaar, June 1971.
"The Cup of Coffee" first appeared in *Ladies' Home Journal,*
July 1973.
"Marley's Chain" first appeared in *House and Garden,*
December 1980.
"Sketches of the Nineteen Seventies" first appeared, in part,
as "Stories of Death and Society" in the *New York*
magazine, July 23, 1973.

To McGeorge Bundy,
with affection and admiration

Contents

Narcissa and Other Fables

Narcissa

$\mathcal{E}$LISE AND SAM MARCY had been regarded somewhat in the light of pioneers when they had sold their Richard Morris Hunt French Renaissance mansion on East Sixtieth Street, in 1922, and moved into a new apartment house at 1000 Fifth Avenue. This vast cube, with its square, regular, marble-silled windows, had been the earliest serious effort to lure the rich from their urban châteaux to a way of living that did not require limitless servants and incessant cleaning, that gave them light and air instead of the cluttered, gleaming, knickknacky darkness that an older generation had regarded as synonymous with a first position. The Marcy apartment, covering the whole of the top two stories, had a panoramic view of Central Park.

Elise's high-roofed studio occupied the street and avenue corner of both stories. It was painted white, and the bookcases between the windows, running from ceiling to floor, reachable in the upper shelves only by a moving ladder, were a golden gleam of old folios of art books. On the two windowless sides of the chamber hung four large portraits of Elise: a Bellows showing her reclining on a divan in yellow pajamas; a Sargent interpreting a rustic mood in a white tennis dress by a garden pool; a Luks concentrating on the small green hat that she happened to be wearing; and a Boldini, an explosion of fantastic fashion, all bare arms and shoulders, twisting, turning, a houri at a Fifth Avenue costume ball.

Elise, at forty-two, liked to think of herself as a *belle laide*. She was tall and skinny, with finely rounded shoulders and full, low-hanging breasts. She even emphasized her angularity in the jerkiness of her motions; her stride was long, her slipper heels absurdly high, her dresses as skin-tight as the fashions would allow. She had a habit of twisting her shoulders as she incessantly smoked, always using a long jade-green holder, but she also affected poses of stillness and mystery when she appeared to be offering a glimpse of depths behind her nervous action.

Something deep, anyway, seemed to be behind her long contemplation of the three Indians posing for her now, arrayed as chiefs. Mr. Pumfax, from the agency, discreetly silent, peeked from time to time at the large unfinished canvas, destined for a post office on Bleecker Street, that was to depict the purchase of Manhattan by the Dutch.

"Of course, I don't have the councilmen in yet," she explained to him. "You will have to get me three other models for them. That should be much easier, of course. Almost any three middle-aged men will do. The costume does the trick. But the Indians are children of nature. The more of their flesh we see, the better. Do you know what my message in this mural will be, Mr. Pumfax?"

"To show the march of progress? The redemption of a wild land from savages?"

"No doubt the officials in the post office will see it that way. But I should like to think that some of my viewers might wonder if the sale of the island was not actually a step backwards. That it is the Dutch who represent the forces of cupidity and the Indians who are the brave and innocent. That that new world may have been lost before it had fairly started!"

Mr. Pumfax gave his patroness the humble look of those whose role it is to confine themselves to the here and now. "The post office will be proud to have an Elise Marcy," he murmured noncommittally.

"Even if she's a frustrated Michelangelo? How can I hope to convey a sense of the power of that world without a nude? Without muscles and thighs and palpitating skin?"

The agent's air of muted respect was all that he could offer to the rich and mighty. Impatiently, Elise continued: "Do you know how the French artist David conveyed *his* sense of the nude under the heavy costumes of his historical canvases? He sketched his models first undraped and then draped them!" She pointed to the tallest of the Indians, who was undressed from the waist up, his back covered with cascading feathers. "That man would have strode to the wall of New Amsterdam, splendidly bare, a symbol of the virility of his tribe. Do you think he would pose for me so?"

Mr. Pumfax blushed in dismay. "But, Mrs. Marcy, these are not professional models! I had to go out and find real Indians for this job. I couldn't possibly ask any of them to disrobe. I . . ."

"Hush, man!"

It was the big Indian who had spoken, in a deep, resonant voice. His injunction was neither abrupt nor impatient; it was simply firm. As the agent stared, gaping, he calmly untied his drawstring and then, with slow deliberation, stepped out of his dropped buckskin trousers. Folding his arms superbly across his chest, he turned to Elise, as fine a nude as she had foreseen.

"I am ready now, ma'am," he said with a grave bow, "to sell you the island."

Elise sent him what she hoped was a dazzling smile as she grabbed her sketchbook to go rapidly to work.

* * *

She had always liked to work with nudes, and her reason was a special one. She wanted to imagine herself in the position of the model; she loved to shiver at the fantasy of a public exposure. She was proud of her own figure, yet at the same time, by the quick click of her departing step, by her habit of black leather and broad tight belts, she seemed to enjoy proclaiming it out of bounds. Men, and women too, stripped for Elise Pierce Marcy, but she disrobed for none. Even Sam Marcy had been able to possess her only in the dark.

She had grown up a kind of haughty princess in a complacent, indulgent, bourgeois environment. The Pierces, Marcys and Farleys, having derived their fortunes from the same western mine, had moved upon New York as a phalanx in the early eighties, confronting Fifth Avenue with what was almost a small rival society. The first generation had been left pretty much to their unlovely and unpolished selves, but the second, including Elise's parents and Sam's, had been accepted in what seemed more like a merger than the scaling of any hierarchical peak.

As her large family — parents, siblings, cousins, uncles, aunts — had been uniformly placid, amiable and dull, Elise, endowed with a darting mind and a perfervid imagination, had languished as a child in lacquered solitude. Everyone liked and admired her, but didn't they equally like and admire each other? In an atmosphere of endless villas with windows opening on endless lawns, of guest-book pages covered with verses and silly drawings, in a seeming infinity of sports and sails and games, she had built for herself the image of a larger future. She was going to use everything that she had to hand — the position, the money, the family itself — to create something bigger.

But what?

Well, she would write poetry, or novels; she would sculpture or paint or even go on the stage. She would collect. She might even be an acrobat! She took expensive lessons in everything from the viola to Hindustani; she filled her diary with effusions and wrote long passionate letters to her closest girlfriends. Everyone murmured how brilliant Elise was, but some of the aunts began to wonder if she would make a proper marriage.

But Elise had already faced the fact that this would be necessary, if only to attain independence. Not for her, however, would be the threadbare European peer or the sharp hungry Yankee. To avoid the disaster of being married for her fortune she would have to confine herself to the family circle, and at the age of twenty-one she elected Sam Marcy, the handsomest and most athletic of her cousins, rich but not as rich as she was. Everyone else had wanted him, and they had been a bit surprised at the ease with which she seemed to have acquired him. Only much later did Elise discover that he had married her to please his dying mother, who had feared that he would become wild unless held in the firm grasp of a member of the tribe.

As a matron, she tried art after art. Sam escorted her patiently on European expeditions where she sat at the feet of various masters, and then, when she had settled at last on painting and had made herself a specialist in murals; when their two children, both girls, had graduated from the nursery; when, in short, his role as a husband, at least as he conceived it, seemed to have been executed, he quietly and ineluctably turned what attention and energy was not required for hunting and polo to the tireless pursuit of women.

He offered no excuse for his conduct and turned a deaf ear and a bland smile to all his wife's angry and at times hysterical protests. He would simply point out that with plenty of money and an abundance of habitations, there was no reason that they should not pursue their incompatible interests in an amicable partnership. He offered her the same liberty on which he insisted, stipulating only that, for the sake of their family, neither should cause any open scandal.

It was very hard on Elise. She had acquired the habit of domination. She had always bullied her parents, and she had trained her daughters, governess-raised, to absolute obedience. But she kicked in vain — she broke her toes — against the unyielding Sam. There was nothing she could do to moderate the friendly contempt that she knew he felt for her and for her art. She would always be aware that he did not consider her a full woman, and that a full woman was the only creature, except for a horse, that interested him.

So Elise was left with what she had thought she had needed, art, and, in the years that followed, with what she had thought she had wanted, success.

* * *

On the day before the disrobing of the Indian chief, Elise had had a startling conversation with Perry St. Clare, a septuagenarian English painter, who had expatriated himself in 1914 because, as he unabashedly put it, he could no longer paint in the "hysterically bellicose" attitude of wartime London. He was a first-rate painter, but a monster of egotism, a great bull of a man with mounds of gray hair and sharp, mean little red eyes under looming gray, bushy eyebrows. He despised the world; he despised Elise Marcy and her occasional loans; he despised his poor little chattering rag of a wife; he despised everything, in short, but his art. On this — the crude, dark landscapes, the bulging, muscular nudes, the somehow ominous baskets of fruit — he lavished all the worship of which his ungenerous nature was capable.

Elise's conversation with St. Clare had taken place in her apartment at a buffet supper that she had given after the opening of a show of French postwar painters. St. Clare had taken his hostess aside to discuss his current project with his usual imperviousness to the rest of the company.

"I'm working on a canvas that's meant to be a kind of comment on the great French mistresses of the past. The royal whores. It will suggest Diane de Poitiers. Nude in her bath, with pearls in her hair and one finger pointing to her tit."

"I know those paintings of Diane. I've even got one in the Southampton house."

"Of course you do. That's where I got the idea. I've looked Diane up in the public library. As I had surmised, she didn't care about men. She was frigid. She kept that beautiful body just for herself and her painters. Oh, of course she had to loan it out to her husband and, later on, when she was older, to the ruttish young king. But you can see in her portraits that the only thing she really craved was ocular admiration."

Elise looked at him keenly. "How can you see that?"

"Well, what other lady of that rank ever posed in the nude?"

"Pauline Bonaparte. For Canova."

He smiled. "She was only a wop, a nobody. She'd have as soon been bare-ass as in court dress."

"Then there are all those ladies by Mignard."

"Just exposed breasts. I don't count them."

"And, of course, Goya's *maja desnuda*."

He laughed disconcertingly. "I knew it! You know them all! Will you do something for me, Elise? Pose in the nude!"

She gasped. "For your Diane?"

"For my Diane."

"You think I'm like her?"

"What does that matter? I want to make it a great painting! A fantasy of a castrating female. A glorious, icy bitch! Will you do it?"

She felt that her eyes must be glittering. "Yes!"

Was it really she who had said that? Was it really her monosyllable that had been uttered in that rasp? But he nodded, as if her acquiescence were the simplest thing in the world.

"Can you come to my studio tomorrow?"

"In the afternoon, perhaps. At three?"

"Don't be late. We won't have much sun. I can get it started, anyway."

And he lunged off to the bar, leaving her transfixed. Had she been actually hypnotized by those despising little red eyes?

* * *

At noon, after Elise's session with the Indian models, her sparkling, sputtering, yellow and black Hispano Suiza drew up before
the two amalgamated brownstones that formed Miss Bacon's
School for Girls on Madison Avenue, and the car's owner, without waiting for the chauffeur, opened the back door for herself
and jumped out to stride rapidly, a tall, swishing movement of
black, into the building. She would pick up her daughters to take
them for lunch at their grandmother's and make use of the occasion to pay a short call, as a trustee of the school, on Miss Bacon.
The headmistress, rising to greet her, thin, pale, attentive, assumed
at once that look to which Elise was so well accustomed, the one
that combined the deference to wealth with the prickly need not
to be "kicked around."

"I've gone over my schedule," Elise started right off, "and I
think that if you decide to establish an art class for the twelfth
grade, I could undertake to teach it one hour a week. It might
be best if the class met in my studio. I can provide a bus."

"We have it under careful consideration. But there has been
no decision as yet."

"What's holding it up? It seems to me that my offer to under-
write the new teacher's salary should answer any objections."

"It's not that, Mrs. Marcy. Everyone appreciates your great
generosity. And I think most of our parents would consider it a
privilege to have their daughters under the tutelage of such a
great artist and, if I may say so, such a great lady."

"Most?"

Miss Bacon hesitated. "I'm afraid this is going to be difficult
for me to say."

"Nothing should be difficult for a headmistress to say."

"Well, I'm afraid, Mrs. Marcy, that some of our mothers are
a bit restricted in their views. The penalty of fame is being famous. They all know your murals. Some have the feeling that
the presence of undraped or partially undraped figures in them is

too suggestive for our girls. There was even talk that you might institute a life class . . . perhaps even with a male model . . .''

"That's perfectly ridiculous. I'd never do such a thing. Who are these mothers, anyway?"

"Well, of course I can't mention names."

"Can't you? Anyway, I'm sure they belong to the newer families. No one with the smallest degree of social security would think her daughter in danger with *me*."

"Actually, Mrs. Marcy, the strongest objector was a member of one of our oldest families."

"Well, it shows what a sorry state we've come to, then. But tell your proper mamas they need have no further concern. I withdraw my suggestion for an art class, as well as my offer to fund it."

"Oh, please, Mrs. Marcy, that is going much too far! We hadn't decided anything yet."

"But I have," Elise retorted as she rose. "Are my daughters ready now?"

She found May and Lucy waiting for her in the hall, large, blonde, giggling girls in the green blouses and hideous green bloomers of the school uniform who followed her without a word to the Hispano, for all the world like two docile sheepdogs. Elise was fond of them, but they did not interest her. They were awed by her; they were good-hearted and earnest, with the fine health and rather bovine equanimity of their grandmother, but, also like Mrs. Pierce, they were literal-minded and conventional.

"Your Aunt Hilda will be at lunch at Granny's," she told them in the car, where both girls occupied the jump seats, leaving the back to Elise and her Siamese cat. "Remember, no remarks about German war atrocities."

"Oh, Mummie, of course not!"

"Oh, Mummie, never!"

Elise leaned back in the seat and half-closed her eyes as she stroked Sophonisba. A vision of what she would be doing that very afternoon superimposed itself between her and the girls. She blinked to shut it out. There was no possible connection between them and her afternoon.

Old Mrs. Pierce lived in a smaller version of the Pitti Palace on Fifty-seventh Street and Fifth Avenue. She and her late husband had shed the rough manners of the parental California settlers, but they had never learned, like their children, the habit of sneering. Mrs. Pierce believed that her Medician palazzo and the French château of her brother across the street were symbols of a financial and moral leadership in which all good Americans believed. It was one of Elise's filial preoccupations to maintain the old lady's illusions.

Although she could never have allowed herself to be so stuffy as to live in a mansion like her mother's, Elise secretly loved it, from its facade of immense stone blocks and arched windows, massively barred, to its dark, cool interior, effulgent with ebony and silver and bronze. She always experienced a delicious little shiver of security as the great grilled doors opened before her into the redeeming gloom, and she reverted to her girlhood, coming home from the mockeries of schoolmates to the silent respectfulness of loyal, elderly servitors. She paused now, sending her daughters ahead to greet their grandmother, while she conferred with Grange, the butler. It had been agreed since her mother's first mild stroke that she should keep an eye on the household.

"Tell Mrs. Kean to bring the green account book to my father's study."

"She's already put it on the desk there, ma'am. Shall I tell her to come down?"

"No. Just the book. Thanks."

She had only wanted an excuse to be in her father's study for a minute alone. It was even darker than the rest of the house, and, if possible, even cleaner. Gold glinted; enamels gleamed.

Sets of unread but daily dusted volumes of classic authors faced her mournfully, patiently. Her mother, in conscious or unconscious emulation of Queen Victoria, kept everything just as it had been when "Mr. Pierce," as she always referred to him, even to his grandchildren, had died.

Elise hardly glanced at the green account book set carefully upon the black mahogany desk, its sides exactly parallel to those of the spotless blotter. There was only one thing that she had come to look at: Gérôme's *Slave Market in Algiers* over the mantelpiece. She stepped forward now to light the bulb that illuminated it.

Facing a crowd of Arab men, some curious, some lustful, some simply appraising, all, under the circumstances, cruel, stood a young woman, her back to the viewer, quite naked, one arm folded to cover her eyes, the other taut with pride and indignation at her side. At her feet lay the rumpled robe from which she had been obliged to step when her turn had come to hear her charms inventoried by the auctioneer. One imagined that she was some great lady, captured at sea by pirates, whose distant family, in Flanders or London or Copenhagen, had been unable to pay the ransom or perhaps simply unaware of her fate. One could imagine the kind of services that would be required by her purchaser, but her stance of outrage only enhanced her attraction. The luminous alabaster of her back suggested an angel in hell.

But to Elise the woman's fate was simply ecstasy. She identified, richly and languorously, with the exposed beauty. She even imagined to herself the shame that the girl might feel at the excitement and thrill of her exposure, and she fancied that very shame as sharply intensifying the delight. The staring eyes of the men pierced her, filled her, thrilled her. She could hear the auctioneer calling attention to details of her body. Who would buy her?

Elise turned now from the picture, her head aching with the violence of her identification with the alabaster slave. She sat down at the desk and opened the green account book without making the smallest effort to take in the figures. After some minutes of blankly staring at the neatly inscribed numerals, she jumped up and went into the dining room to take her seat at the long, silver-laden table, at her mother's right and opposite her sister. Lucy and May made up the silent ends of the horseshoe.

"You are so good to help with the accounts, dear Elise," her mother murmured. "You are so lucky to have your poor dear father's head for figures. I don't know what I should do without you."

Elise smiled. It was absurd how much it gratified her to be the favorite child of this tiny, plain, dumpy woman who looked like a cook on her day off and who would not have distinguished between a Sargent and a Perry St. Clare. But what other human being had ever really loved her? Elise sometimes felt that if anything should happen to her mother she would simply die herself.

As Mrs. Pierce now unfolded to her granddaughters, in tedious detail, the roll of their mother's efficiencies, Elise, her eyes half-closed, felt her heart miss a beat as her mind leaped a quarter of a century into the past to that bright day and dancing blue sea of Newport when she had caught her mother in her bedroom reading her diary. She had snatched it away angrily to glance at the entry at which it was opened: "I hate her, I hate her, I hate her!" Their interchange still rang in her ears.

"How *dare* you read my diary?"

"You wrote that you hated me!" There were tears in her mother's eyes. Her little round face seemed red and swollen.

"But you wouldn't let me ask Tommy Starks to the clambake! You said he'd been born when his parents had only been married three months!"

"That doesn't mean you can hate me."

"You've never tried to understand me! Nobody has! Nobody cares!"

"You still shouldn't hate me."

Elise had had to hug her and hug her to be forgiven. But she had never been quite forgiven. The hurt had been too deep. And it had been worth it in the long thereafter to have learned that where a husband and children, where all the cousins, all the friends, had failed Elise, there should still have existed that homely, patient mother's love, unaffected by a daughter's brilliance or a daughter's temperament, indifferent to everything but rejection.

Elise shuddered now at the sudden image of her mother watching her in St. Clare's studio. But no, that was not an unimaginable thought. There had to be two layers of existence. There *had* to be!

"Oh, Mother, darling, you don't really need anyone to help you with the housekeeping books!" she exclaimed suddenly, causing her daughters to start. "Everyone knows you're the most competent woman in the world."

Mrs. Pierce shook her head gravely, taking the compliment at its face value. She had no natural vanity; she considered herself important only because the world did. Elise knew that her mother would have been perfectly content on a porch rocker in a small western town, boasting to her neighbors about her children. But she had accepted a more regal fate submissively, even with a kind of humility. She sat in her box through long German operas that she neither liked nor understood and presided over evening receptions that bored all but the most avid social climbers.

Hilda, Countess von Berwitz, had none of her older sister's charm or talent; there was no *belle* to qualify the *laide*. Like the ex-Kaiser's late mother, she trumpeted her homeland in Berlin and Berlin in her homeland and found herself unpopular on both sides of the Atlantic. Thin, cold, with suspicious eyes and a long drippy nose, she peered about the table.

"I shall certainly need your mother to instruct me if I visit any art galleries on this trip," she advised her nieces. "This modern art is a mystery to me! And the things people hang in their homes today! It's really alarming. I was at Sophie Burnbow's yesterday, where everything used to be so pleasant and homey. But you wouldn't believe what she's put up over her mantelpiece. A Perry St. Clare! She said she got it cheap because there's so little market for him now. He's dreadfully fallen off, is he not, Elise?"

Elise looked bleakly at her sister. She knew that Hilda was perfectly aware that St. Clare was a charter member of what she smirkingly called Elise's "court."

"Perry can always be counted on to change his style if there's any danger of its becoming popular," she retorted coolly. "But how many painters do you know who are capable of a new vision at seventy-three? What does your friend Sophie's painting depict?"

"I believe it's called David and Jonathan. But you'd hardly guess it was from Scripture. There are two very large, very naked men on a red beach before a green sea under a blue cloud. One doesn't know where it is ... Greece, perhaps? But why Greece? St. Clare is an Englishman, isn't he?"

"He is. One of the reasons he came here is that he admires American painters. He finds them more vital than the English."

"You mean he likes the 'ashcan school'?" The countess glanced at her nieces as if to take them into her joke.

"Just so," snapped Elise.

"Well, the way his David places a hand on Jonathan's shoulder! One really wonders just what St. Clare was trying to imply." The countess looked from Elise to her mother, her sudden silence seeming to imply that the subject of homosexuality could hardly be brought up before the girls.

"Probably nothing more than the newspapers meant to imply, a few years back, between your former emperor and Philipp zu Eulenburg."

"The emperor had nothing to do with that filth!" cried the countess, instantly wrathful. "No matter what your scandal sheets may have had to say about it!"

" 'Your'?"

"Yes, your. I am no longer American when it comes to things like that. Really, Elise! I begin to see why it is that some of Miss Bacon's mothers have doubts about your proposed art class!"

"Oh, you've heard that, have you? I thought it had a Teutonic ring. I shouldn't wonder if you put the idea in their stupid heads!"

"Girls, girls!" Mrs. Pierce was not sorry for the chance to resume her maternal sway. The great ladies of culture and Kultur had gone so far beyond her that it was pleasant to have them revert, for a moment anyway, to the scratching, hair-pulling creatures they once had been. "Elise, you must remember that your daughters are present. And, Hilda, you should keep in mind that in this country people are accustomed to speak of the Kaiser in a way that makes Elise's remarks seem like compliments!"

"But it's still slander, what she said, Mama!"

"Even so, my dear. It is not tactful of Elise to repeat it, and it is not prudent of you so sharply to resent it. Let us turn to other topics. What do people in Germany think of this terrible police strike in Boston?"

* * *

Elise huddled behind the canvas curtain that sheltered a corner of Perry St. Clare's cluttered studio on top of a four-story house in Christopher Street. She had taken off her clothes and put on a silk red robe. She stepped out now to face the old man's appraising stare.

"Is that your idea of nudity?"

"Your studio is not so warm that I care to increase the time that I am exposed. Let me know when you're ready."

"I'm ready now! Would you kindly take that dreadful red rag off and recline on that couch? Your hands behind your neck, please. In the pose of Goya's *maja*."

"Is that how you see me?"

"Just do as I say, if you don't mind. I take it you want to be treated like a professional model."

"Don't you treat everyone that way? We're all used to your manners, Perry."

It was now time. She could delay no longer. She could dress, of course, and take her leave. The Hispano was waiting below. But no, she would not be such a fool. Quickly, almost violently, she stripped off the robe and let it fall to the ground about her feet as in the Gérôme. Then, with a sudden, almost involuntary gesture, she covered her eyes with her left arm. It was as if the very air had eyes. She shivered deliciously. But I'm enjoying it! she thought in surprise. I'm actually enjoying something that I anticipated enjoying!

"What the hell sort of pose is that?" came the gruff voice.

"It's the *Slave Market*. Gérôme." She dropped her arm, embarrassed. "It's in my father's study. I used to love it as a girl."

"Gérôme! You dare mention that name in my studio? I'll have to have the place fumigated."

"All right, Perry. I'll go to work."

The leather on the couch was cold against her shoulders and buttocks. But still, the pose was not uncomfortable. Perry had turned on an electric heater, and she felt the beams warm against her left side. But the first fine shock of the experience had faded already. She began to wonder if it would turn out to be like a doctor's examination. Perry was working with rapid strokes at his charcoal sketch. Would she be bored? Would that be all?

But then he said something that made a difference; she was excited again.

"You have a good figure for a gal your age. It's a pity you keep it covered up all the time."

"Ah, you *see* that!"

"Doesn't it feel more alive than when you're swathed in furs, getting in and out of limousines? Isn't it more fun to wiggle a bare ass at some feller?"

Elise felt her throat tighten pleasantly. "But I'm not wiggling my ass."

"We'll do a rear view later." He drew for some minutes in silence. Then he changed the subject abruptly, dismayingly. "How would you like another opportunity to encourage the arts? I could sure use a thousand bucks."

"Oh, Perry. Again?" The Algerian marketplace disintegrated.

"Frankly, Elise, I'm in a jam. I need it right away."

"What for, this time?"

"What's it to you? You'd pay more than that for a wedding present for some cousin you didn't even know."

"But I gave you a thousand only last month! And three thousand last year. You talk about encouraging the arts! I'd only be encouraging you to drink and gamble."

"If you could see yourself! Moralizing in the nude!"

"I'm not moralizing," Elise retorted, disconcerted. "I'm being realistic. I have supported a great many artists . . ."

"Nobody's questioning your generosity in the past, Elise. It's your future that seems to be in doubt."

"I hardly call it generosity to hand out money to every bartender in Christopher Street!"

"Goddamnit, woman, I have debts to pay!"

"Suppose, then, I give the money to your wife?"

Perry stamped his feet. "If you try to humiliate me, Elise Marcy, I'll kick your ass out of this studio."

"Is that humiliating you? To ask for some assurance that the money will actually get to your creditors? Do you think your record has been such that I should put a blind faith in you?"

"There speaks the daughter of Wall Street! Pah! You stink of money. It comes out of your every pore. Cover yourself up — put on that gown — *do* something. Please!"

Trembling with anger, Elise sprang to her feet and hastily slipped back into her robe. She turned to him briskly now, as she vigorously tied the belt.

"I should like to know what makes you think you have the right to plunge your greedy paw into my pocketbook every time you're bust!"

"Because I'm a genius!" And then, for a moment anyway, he seemed actually to relent. "Oh, all right. So I like to drink. So I sometimes play the horses. What the hell! I'm an old man. But if I can keep on painting for just two or three more years, I may be one of the greats. And what's a few measly thousand bucks to you in return for the privilege of keeping me going? It'll make your name in art history! You like to play Lady Bountiful to the arts. Well, play it!"

"If I treated every artist in New York according to the size of his ego, my fortune would be gone in a year's time. Lady Bountiful! You seem to forget I'm an artist, too."

"With those murals? Come off it!"

Elise was used to his abuse, but this shook her. "Of course, you can't see any merit in anyone but Perry St. Clare," she retorted weakly.

"Can't I? I can't see merit in Léger? In Kandinsky? In Rouault? I'm just better, that's all."

"I think I'll get dressed now. And leave you alone with your greatest admirer."

"Wait a minute! I want to finish this sketch."

"I'm sure such a genius can do that without a model."

"But I've got to finish it so you can pay me for it!"

"Pay you for it! There was no agreement about that. If you feel abused, tell your lawyer to see mine."

This last exasperated him beyond all control. "Do you think I don't see the game you're playing?" he roared.

Elise stared at the terrible old man with a sinking heart. "What game is that?"

"Playing queen of the Village in Fifth Avenue and queen of Fifth Avenue in the Village! When you're bored with society, you tell yourself, 'I'm a great painter!' And when you're disgusted with smelly artists and all their crude talk, you tell yourself, 'I could buy and sell the lousy lot of them!' "

Elise, without a word, hurried to find her clothes behind the canvas.

* * *

She sat in the armchair drawn up before Mr. Blair's great, oblong Napoleonic desk, smoking. It was he, the veteran lawyer, the grizzled leader of the bar, small, hirsute, black-garbed, with starey little eyes, who seemed on edge.

"But, er, I don't . . . I don't quite see it. You say you were posing . . . in . . . in what the children call a 'birthday suit'?"

"I was posing in the nude, Mr. Blair. A service that one professional artist is glad to render another."

"Mr. St. Clare does not seem to see it that way," Mr. Blair continued, turning back to the letter that Elise had given him.

"Mr. St. Clare sees it as an opportunity to blackmail me, as that letter makes abundantly clear. He says that if I don't loan him the money he asked for, he will offer the finished sketch to my husband."

"And do you think he will do that?"

"We must assume he will."

"Under the circumstances, I think you should authorize me to negotiate the purchase of the sketch."

"But he could simply draw another!"

"What evidence is there that you posed for him?"

She paused to consider this. "It doesn't matter!" she said at last, shaking her head impatiently. "Because I'd never stoop to deny it. But if it ever got out, it would kill my mother. Isn't there some way we can frighten St. Clare? He's an alien, you know. And a blackmailer. Couldn't he be deported?"

Mr. Blair's eyes glinted. He had done his perfunctory duty in recommending a settlement. Now he could do what he loved above all things: strike down the presumptuous with the clubs of the rich and mighty. "I think I could induce the police to seize the sketch. One of our partners is very close to the commissioner. And if St. Clare raises a howl, we simply institute deportation proceedings. Yes, I think we can handle him."

"Good. And what do I do?"

"Nothing."

"Not even answer the letter?"

"Not even answer the letter."

Elise nodded. Mr. Blair would savage her opponent and would enjoy doing it. Oh, she could count on that! The man who had first stripped her and then insulted her would learn his lesson. She rose and gave the lawyer a final injunction.

"If Mr. Marcy must learn the facts, be sure it is *I* who tell him!"

In the reception hall, to which Mr. Blair now escorted her, Elise paused, suddenly struck, before a painting that she had not observed when she came in. It showed a strip of hillside, green between clumps of autumn woods, descending to a slaty gray pond under an ash-white sky.

"A St. Clare!" she exclaimed. "Where on earth did you get it?"

"Don't you remember? Your husband was good enough to give it to me two Christmases ago. But my dear wife, I fear, has little eye for modern painting. I decided it would be better to hang it down here. It's a view in Kent, I believe."

"Dorset."

She walked over to the painting and remained for several minutes standing before it. What was the miracle that Perry performed with that simple scene? How did he take it out of Dorset, out of England, out of actuality, and make it so strangely independent? Why did that green paint, that blotchy sky, make her heart leap?

"I'll tell you one thing, Mr. Blair. That old man can paint."

"I assume that of anyone you have patronized."

"I would give my right index finger — I would chop it off right now, in front of you — if I could paint that sky."

"That sky! But it's just a daub of white. Why, Mrs. Marcy, you're twenty times the artist St. Clare is!"

Elise turned to look searchingly into the lawyer's eyes. He actually meant it!

"Don't do anything about Perry St. Clare," she said, suddenly depleted. "Forget this visit. I shall go home now and send him his thousand dollars."

Blair gaped. "And the picture? The picture... er ... of you?"

But Elise Marcy, despite the blows to her ego of the past twenty-four hours, was still a woman of quick decision and imperious gesture. Perhaps these qualities were all that would be left her. Well, then, she would make do with them! "He can keep it," she said with a snort and strode to the door.

The Seagull

*D*EAR BISHOP PINE:

You are probably aware by now that my vestry has voted my demission as rector of St. Andrews Church in Oyster Cove. I do not know if you are also aware that my wife, Ann, has left me. And now this letter will bring you the latest development of the whole sad story: my own decision to give up holy orders. I fear it is irrevocable. But because of my long admiration of you, because of the inspiration which you afforded me as my dean at divinity school, and because of my two wonderful years with you in the cathedral, I feel that I owe you an exact account of what has happened. Who knows? My sorry state may not be untypical. There may be others who, with your help and guidance, will profit by my experience.

I sometimes think that I should never have left the cathedral. Certainly I was very happy there — perhaps too happy. Such may not be the healthiest state of a clergyman. But I was so proud to believe that we were in the vanguard of affirmative action! All around us was the gray picture of urban desolation: poverty, drugs, crime, broken families without hope or faith. And even farther to the east, where the city was wealthy and where philanthropists and liberals were to be found, it was the philanthropy of the materialist, the liberalism of the agnostic. I felt as the apostle must have felt in a pagan world; you were my

Saint Paul. When you invited the ballet to dance in the cathedral, when you led that peace march down Broadway, when you ordained the lesbian priest, I felt that the Episcopal Church was living again in Christ.

Ann was less exalted than I about your innovations. She was even frankly relieved when we received our call to Oyster Cove. But I had grave misgivings. I had yearned for a stiffer challenge: for a parish in East Harlem or in the poorest area of the Deep South. It was you who persuaded me that there was just as great a need of salvation on the north shore of Long Island as in indigent places — perhaps more. And of course it was also true, as you pointed out, that the church must never neglect her sources of financial support. A priest is a soldier; he must go where he is called.

Things started well enough in Oyster Cove. My new parishioners turned out in brave array to see me conduct my first service in that quaint little Romanesque church nestled in the wooded triangle bordered by three vast estates. Although the community could hardly be called a religious one, there was a definite interest in the church as an integral part of the structure of society. One must, after all, have weddings, christenings, funerals! Oh, I know, Bishop. I hear your gentle reminder: "Don't knock what you've got. *Build* on it!" Well, I tried to.

I introduced myself in my first sermon. I told them I had a wife, with whom I was passionately in love; two children, seven and nine, who seemed not unpromising; a canary, an Airedale, and an old macaw, which looked fierce but wasn't. I told them how I stood on women's rights, gay lib, pot, capital punishment, and strip mining. They seemed to take it all very well. Even if they weren't liberal, they showed signs of approving a liberal minister. It has perhaps become the fashion. One jolly old vestryman went so far as to nudge me in the ribs after the service and whisper in a hoarse voice that all could hear: "That's right, boy.

Tell 'em about you and your pretty young wife. Sex always works, even in church. The old gals lap it up!" I wonder if this should have been my warning.

At any rate, I considered the auspices good. Christ expects us to use every tool that we find to hand. Attendance went up; the contribution plate was gratifyingly full. And it was wonderful to see my Ann so happy. She and the children adored Oyster Cove and flourished in the country air. Even our Airedale seemed not to miss the rich urban street smells.

But the work troubled me, or rather, I should say, the lack of work. There were no poor in the parish. There were few old people, and almost no unmarried ones. It was a commuting society; after sixty-five one retired to New England or Florida, and the unwed clung to the city. Oh, there were things I could do, of course, in the village of Oyster Cove proper (as opposed to the suburban community), and I worked closely with the other churches, particularly the Roman Catholic, but it concerned me that my parish calls seemed to be treated as social events. The husbands were never at home for them, and the children were likely to be sent outside or to the rumpus room to play. The lady of the house, dressed as for a Sunday service, would receive me formally and then relax, over tea or even a cocktail, to discuss everybody's problems but her own. I supposed that it would take a while before they would trust me with anything more personal. After all, they belong to an age where the priest's function has largely been taken over by the psychiatrist. I had to be patient.

When I met Jessie Hamill, I thought that perhaps my real job was at last beginning. She was a large, fair woman of thirty-seven or -eight, who might have been almost beautiful had she taken off twenty pounds. She had come to the parish house to offer her services as a volunteer. She would do anything; time hung on her hands. Her position was a sad but not uncommon one for that community: her husband, a computer analyst, a handsome and popular man, had deserted her to marry his young secretary, with whom he now lived in the city. There were two children, both in boarding school, a barely adequate alimony, and a bleak void where there had been a happy hearth. Mrs. Hamill seemed intelligent and objective in presenting her facts. I should add that she did not bring them out until I had questioned her.

"The whole thing was too ghastly to seem quite real," she explained with a dry little smile and a faint shrug. "You see, I had no inkling of what was coming. Not so much as a hint. You will say I must have been blind. Very well, I was blind. It never crossed my mind that I didn't have the happiest marriage in Oyster Cove until the day Mike telephoned to tell me to meet him for dinner at Quo Vadis. Well, poor unsuspecting me, who adores French restaurants, of course I dropped everything and rushed into town. Imagine my feelings when — I had hardly downed my first cocktail — he hit me smack in the face with the news that he was in love. 'Madly' in love."

"But that's a common delusion at his age," I pointed out. "The last desperate clutch at youth. It's not your fault."

"Fault?" Her laugh was sharp, faintly mocking. It seemed to make a bit of a fool of me, but not invidiously. "I didn't even exist to have a fault. He *was* in love, and for the first time, too. What had *I* been? Puberty, puppy love, sentimentality, you name it. And the horrible thing is that I'm beginning to think he did right. The last time I talked to him, when he came to pick up the kids on Christmas Eve, he said, 'Jess, I know I've been a heel, but what's a man to do? I'm happy now. I didn't know what happiness was before. That's not a reproach. For me it all simply depended on Ellen, and I hadn't met Ellen. So now I work better, play better, feel better. Damn it all, I'd do it again! We've only got one life.' "

"But how long will his newfound happiness last?"

"Forever!" She flung up her hands in a sarcastic gesture of

despair. "That's the hell of it. The girl is charming, and she adores him. But where does it all leave me? With my life over, I'm afraid. I used to believe my function was simply to be Mike's wife. Well, now I'm not his wife. The church recognizes his new marriage. I suppose God, if he exists, does, too. Get a job, people say. Sure. But I'm not trained for anything, and my springs are busted."

"You put your case very clearly. I wonder if you couldn't teach. How about trying your hand with the Sunday School? We're going to be doing it all over."

"Well, I don't know my Old Testament, and I . . ."

"Oh, we go very light on the Bible these days," I assured her. "The emphasis is all on ethics and social service."

She looked at me now, as with a sudden, timid hope. "Would *you* help me? I mean, could I see you every so often? To talk, like this? I think you might help. I think you might understand."

"But of course. What else am I here for?"

Ann was very skeptical that night when I told her of our talk. "*I* hear she drinks."

"It wouldn't be surprising, under the circumstances, would it?"

"But I mean before. Before he left her. They say he got tired of having to keep an eye on her at parties."

"We must be charitable, darling. Any way you look at it, the woman needs help."

Ann's gray eyes showed a steely look. "Watch your step, big boy. That's all I have to say."

"And just what do you mean by that?"

"What do you *think* I mean?"

Ann was always very possessive about me, and I decided to ignore her remark. But I remembered what she had said about Jessie's drinking when on two Sunday mornings in succession the latter failed to turn up for her class. I was all the more disappointed in that she had started so well, with a small group of serious teenagers whose interest she had excited in an initial session on "the pros and cons of cohabitation." I decided to drive over and call on her.

There was something desolate about the house. Its style was what is called "developer's Queen Anne," and it sat on two bare acres of lawn and field, with no trees, no garden, and an empty swimming pool. It was a home whose only excuse would have been children playing in it and around it, as the netless basketball hoop over the door of the attached garage seemed poignantly to imply. I found Mrs. Hamill alone, and she made no effort to whisk away the cocktail tray by the sofa. Shrugging, she poured me a drink from the shaker.

"I know I've been rotten about the class," she admitted. Her voice was steady enough, but the syllables were the least bit blurred. "A week ago, I learned that both my children were planning to go west this summer to a ranch with their father. Of course, it's quite natural for them to want to go, but I can't help it — it's knocked me for a loop. They were very sweet, and offered to give up the trip if I really minded, but I couldn't accept that. So there we are, Denis. I *may* call you Denis? Thank you." She paused to stare at me for a long moment. Her expression seemed caught between her own now frankly accepted despair and a rather bemused curiosity about what my reaction to it would be. "Will it shock you too much if I tell you that I can't think of one good reason not to take my own life?"

"I can give you a reason!" I exclaimed with instant passion. "It will hurt Jesus Christ! Do you want to do that?"

She looked at me in astonishment. "But of course I don't believe any of that."

"I can *make* you believe it!"

"How?"

"Suppose I come here, say twice or three times a week, and talk to you for half to three-quarters of an hour? On a regular basis? Would you let me?"

"But what would your wife say?"

"She knows it's my job."

Jessie actually laughed. "Dear me. Well, I'll try to make it something less than that." Then, as quickly, she was grave again. "Seriously, Denis, you're an angel. Maybe literally."

When I got home that evening I told Ann about my project with a promptitude that indicated less assurance about her attitude than I had professed to Jessie. As it turned out, any assurance at all would have been folly. Ann was simply furious.

"That drunken slut!" she cried. "How can you be such an ass? Don't you see she's making a play for you? And don't kid yourself it's because of your *beaux yeux,* either. It's because she's bored and lonely and bitchy!"

"Darling, you're not only being unkind, you're being unwise. That woman is on the verge of suicide."

"Well, I wish somebody'd push her over!"

"Now you're being un-Christian," I said mildly.

"I don't even know that I *am* a Christian!" Ann retorted hotly. "All I know is that I'm not going to loan you out to a designing hussy."

"But surely you'll admit it's the duty of a priest to look after lost souls? That woman is the first serious challenge I've had in Oyster Cove. If I fail her I may as well pack my bags and go back to the cathedral."

"All right, then, look after her. But look after yourself, too. And look after your marriage." Ann's chin, thrust forward, had a harsh, angular look. "Christian duty may be your concern, but my family's mine. To me it's God and Trinity and all the life hereafter I'm ever going to need. That may come as a shock to you, Denis Sanders, but there's something else you'd better learn too. No matter how important my marriage is to me, it's not worth a compromise. The first funny business between you and that lush, and I'm through!"

Of course, it was thus that she established in my mind the idea that my relationship with Jessie Hamill might have a sexual basis. Had this not come simultaneously with the revelation that Ann considered herself only formally a Christian, it might not have had such an impact. But as things were, I reeled under her double barrage. First she smeared my function as a priest; then she stripped our union of its sanctity. Evidently she could see me as nothing but a rooster, strutting through the barnyard in search of a hen. What were the Gospels, what was the Sermon on the Mount, what was Christ Himself but a cock-a-doodle-doo? But when I pointed this out to her, she would not yield an inch. She simply repeated stonily what she had said.

"Why have you waited until now to tell me all this?" I asked in despair.

"Because there's never been another woman before."

"You think there's one now?"

"I think there's one after *you* now. And I'm taking no chances."

What was finally decided between us took the form of a treaty. I was to be allowed to visit Jessie Hamill on Wednesdays and Saturdays at five o'clock for a trial period of three weeks. I was to be home promptly at six, and I was not to have a drink while I was there. Finally, I was to inform Jessie of the existence of these terms.

Jessie, to my surprise, seemed amused. She at once agreed to the conditions, and the first two visits went off with absolute propriety. It was a little bit like an hour of therapy. Jessie, at first constrained, rapidly warmed up. She told me volubly of her childhood, her meeting with Mike, his courtship, their early marriage. Indeed, I was inundated with a full tide of reminiscence that seemed to have no spiritual potential. But on the third meeting everything went wrong.

To begin with, she had a visitor when I called. Andy Smithers, a big, red-complexioned man, the largest landowner in

Oyster Cove, the father of seven children and the henpecked husband of the community crosspatch, had evidently been drinking with Jessie most of the afternoon. Both were in a rather bleary state, and Andy stared at me with undisguised hostility and uttered no greeting. It took Jessie ten minutes to make him go, and then she had to walk with him to his car. When she returned she stood for a moment in the doorway to the living room, staring at me in a rather wild, haggard way. She struck me as on the verge of hysteria.

"Andy says people are talking about us!" she exclaimed at last. "I told him you only cared about my soul. Who ever cared about my body? My poor, soggy, too-big body? Could a body like mine have a soul?" She ran her hands feverishly up and down her sides. "I tell you, Denis, I don't exist! I never have! I'm a worthless sot, and I'll be better off dead. Who needs me? Who wants me?" She stamped her foot in a fit of violent temper. "Damn it all, Denis, help me! Can't you *help* me?"

My taking Jessie to bed that afternoon was a perfectly deliberate act. I believed that it was my duty to convince her that she was a live, lovable woman. I considered that the act of sexual union under the circumstances was equivalent to a blood transfusion. In primitive societies the functions of priest and physician were frequently identical; there are times today when they still can be. You will ask if I derived pleasure from the act. Certainly I did. Had I not, I could never have convinced her that she was lovable. I derived and conveyed intense pleasure. But I believed that I was performing a kind of sacrament. When I left Jessie she was calm again, even serene. I returned home by half-past seven and told Ann that I had had to change a tire. I had never been able to lie to her successfully before. I dared to hope that it was God who had given me the necessary fortitude.

You will say that I was making some very bold assumptions, but what happened thereafter seemed to bear out the boldest of them. You know what is commonly supposed to be the inevitable aftermath of such a situation as I have just described. The "other" woman is never satisfied with a single act. She yearns for more, and then more; she berates her lover if he fails to comply; she makes terrible scenes. If he continues to oblige, his life becomes a tissue of lies and subterfuges. In the end his wife discovers all. Who has not read that novel or seen that play?

But that is not what happened. What happened was precisely what I had hoped and prayed would happen. Jessie Hamill pulled herself together, as if by a miracle. She wrote me a letter, which she told me to show to Ann, in which she said that she was so much better that I could now discontinue the twice-weekly visitations. She did not fail again to appear for her Sunday School class, and she made no efforts in the parish house to see me alone. Her attitude in public to both Ann and myself seemed friendly and natural. She told us that she was on a diet to lose thirty pounds. People even said that she was on the wagon. Had I not reason to believe that that carnal act had been spiritually inspired?

The violence of my disillusionment was to equal the fury of my folly. One Sunday afternoon, when I returned from a visit to Cedarhurst, where I had been invited to preach, I found Ann, dressed in her city clothes, waiting grimly for me in the living room. The children were nowhere to be seen.

"Something's happened!" I exclaimed.

"No, but something's going to," she announced in a hard, flat tone. "I'm going to leave you. I'm going to Mother. With the children. Tonight."

I found myself suddenly sitting in a chair, and there was a throb where I had bitten my lip. "May I ask why?"

"You know why. That Hamill woman was here this morning. She told me everything."

"*She* told you? Why, in God's name?"

"Because she was afraid I would hear about it. Andy Smithers parked his car down the road and came back to gawk at you through the window. Then he apparently blurted it all out in Murphy's bar. But you'll be glad to hear he's sorry and that he's expressing his contrition most touchingly. He's left his wife and seven children and is going to marry the old slut." Ann snorted derisively. "I'm sure you're mad with jealousy!"

"I'm not jealous at all," I retorted, beginning now to assemble my wits. "I'm simply saddened that Jessie should be a party to the breakup of a home. There was never any question of love between us."

"Oh, she told me all about that! She told me you'd done it for the good of her soul. She thought *that* would make me forgive you!"

"I don't suppose I've done much for her soul. It's all too horrible. Is Andy really going to divorce his wife?"

"Oh, yes, your Jessie has him firmly on the hook. He'll never shake free of her now. And do you know what she used for bait? You, you poor sap! I got the story from Alice Mellish, after she left. What Jessie needed, you see, was the chance to show Andy that someone else could get the hots for her. He'd been sniffing around her for months, but like so many men these days, he couldn't think any piece of meat was really palatable unless someone else was sniffing it too. A young minister was just what she needed. To show that old Jessie, still the sexpot, could make him break his vows, forget his wife, forget Christ!" Ann rose, almost exultant in her fury. "Oh, she had it all planned out. And how it worked! When Andy saw you two, he decided that she was Venus herself! And now he has to have her, even if it costs him a million bucks to get rid of his wife!"

"But, Ann, if you know *why* I did it, can't you forgive me?"

"Never!" Her voice rose almost to a scream. "If it had been a question of lust, a quick roll in the hay, that might have been different. But *this* way! Oh . . . you disgust me! You nauseate me! Get out of my sight!"

And so she left me. Do you remember your sermon about the seagull? It was the first I ever heard you deliver. You told the story of how you had been out sailing and found a seagull swimming in circles, unable to fly. Its bill was pierced by one barb of a triple fishhook, its wing by another, so the poor bird's head was pinioned back against its side. You told how you picked it up and worked for half an hour to release it. And then what did it do? It ruffled its feathers, gave you a nasty bite, and flew away. You used this as a parable to illustrate the ingratitude that all healers and priests must be prepared to receive. I see now that Jessie Hamill was simply behaving as she believed she had to behave in a suburban society. She had been wounded, and the wounded must look to themselves as best they can or be pecked to death by other birds. Once cured, however, she flapped happily off to rejoin the flock. Her final bite was even kindly meant! There is no reason for me to be bitter. But neither is there any reason for me to go on ministering to this community. And if I cannot minister to one, I am unfit to minister to any.

I know what you are going to tell me: that seagulls, too, have souls. All I can suggest is that you send another seagull to save them!

Cordially yours,
Denis Sanders

The Ghost
of Hamlet's Ghost

FOR FIVE YEARS NOW, really ever since 1965, Marvin Lesterhouse's reputation as a teacher of Shakespeare had been on the skids. At forty-five, at his peak, he had kidded himself that he had achieved an eminence that was at last secure, that he could continue indefinitely to lecture to large classes at the College of Manhattan, holding both the affection and the enthusiasm of his students with his high-pitched, tense, unblushingly lyrical analyses of characters and motivations. He had from the beginning, as he well knew, been subject to the deadly charge of "Bradleyism," of making up early and last chapters for characters of whose lives the bard had furnished us only scanty glimpses — in short, of filling out biographies, of supplying King Lear with a wife and Hamlet with a college career. But he had hoped that he had made up for this by the very intensity of his appreciations, by his aptitude in conveying some of his own sense of beauty to his classes, and that this histrionic capacity might have proved sufficient, in conjunction with his perfectly competent grasp of the symbols, myths, and other jargon of modern criticism, to convince his students that a simple enjoyment of his performance was not necessarily to be condemned as an indulgence in literary nostalgia.

Now, however, no quaver of the voice, no passionate declamation, no wizardry of memory in quotations could avert the stern questions from humorless, unshaven faces, of why all this was "relevant," of what did Imogen or Viola or even Cleopatra have to do with the problems of desegregation or the war in Vietnam. The answer, "Nothing, thank God!" did not long stave off inattention followed by nonattendance, nor did one factitious effort to meet the young men halfway: an improvised lecture on *Troilus and Cressida* in which the noble Trojans, with their good hearts and bad cause, and the wily Greeks, with their duplicity and genuine wrong, had been likened to the Americans and the North Vietnamese. Lesterhouse had been made to feel a thorough fool, the inevitable doom of anachronisms who try to convince others — and themselves — that they are not anachronisms, or even that anachronisms do not exist.

It was all made a great deal worse by the fact that he had, even in his palmy days, suspected some such thing. He had carried about within him — locked up tight, to be sure — a disquieting, even at times a panicky, sense of not being, of not even approaching, really, what he tried so desperately to look like. When he stood on the platform and gravely intoned the Ghost's sepulchral warning in *Hamlet,* did any of his play-acting make the class forget the fair, fat, fiftyish bachelor professor, with the sandy-yellow, graying hair cut short and parted in the middle and the voice that tended to squeak or purr except when it rose to the unexpected thunder of his too rare fits of temper? Did they not jeer at him behind his back and suggest obscene motives for his befriending of this or that nice young man who would come to him after class to ask if Hamlet were really mad or Ophelia really chaste? Had it not always been a harsh, unlaughing world that made only the scantest pretense of having any use at all for people who lived in their imaginations?

During the summer that followed the terrible spring when the dean had cut his courses for the following semester from four to two, Marvin Lesterhouse had suffered a mild nervous collapse. One night he even went so far as to discuss retirement with his sister, Rhoda, who lived with him — or really *on* him (for it was he who had inherited the whole of the whimsical paternal grandfather's fortune) in the big, dark, cool, ugly, beloved brownstone mansion on Brooklyn Heights. Neither of them ever left the city even for a day in the hot months.

"I don't see why you wouldn't be glad to quit," Rhoda observed. "You'd have more time to write."

"Oh, write!" he said impatiently. "Everyone's always talking about writing. Anyone can write. Who needs more books? The great communication is by word of mouth. Think of the millions of books one has read on Shakespeare."

"*I* haven't."

"Well, I mean people in my game," he retorted. "But who made me *feel* him first? Professor Tinker, when I was a freshman at Yale!"

"Yes, but isn't that just what we're discussing? The fact that you're *not* Tinker?"

Rhoda was as plain and stout, as long-nosed and short-haired, as any woman lawyer could be in the mind of a male antifeminist. She was consistently, even persistently, unromantic and literal. If she burped, it had to be a triumphant assertion of the natural over the artificial, never an inadvertent noise that might conceivably be apologized for. She was devoted to Marvin, but she regarded his nervous problems as the anticipatable result of a life not based on the sounder realities.

"You needn't be unkind, Rhoda."

"But I'm only trying to help. Honestly!"

Marvin wondered with a sigh if there was any relationship as arid as that of bachelor brother and old-maid sister. It was a marriage without juice; it had all the rivalry, all the bickering, all the petty meannesses, but none of the exaltation. Rhoda knew that he, at least, *had* his exaltations: with his library, his teaching, his students; and her jealousy was tediously present in her constant hashing over of these things to ferret out what she liked to call the "vicarious" in his life. Poor creature, how happy she would have been with but a whiff of one of his illusions!

"Why don't you give your students Betterton?" she demanded suddenly.

"Betterton?" He gaped. "What do you mean, give them Betterton?"

"Well, you've always been so convinced that you were teaching Shakespeare. You've never listened to me when I've tried to tell you that you were really teaching acting. Styles of acting. Like Thomas Betterton's. It's your 'thing,' as they say today. Well, do it!"

Marvin felt the odd little tension of interest that always accompanies one's recognition that a relative may actually be speaking disinterestedly. For years he had taken for granted that he knew every motive behind every one of his sister's speeches, as he had taken it equally for granted that she knew his. Their conversations had not really been made with words, but with word-like balls, batted back and forth. Yet now he actually had a vision . . . but, of course, he could not yet admit it.

"Would that be 'relevant'?" he asked bleakly.

"It would be different. And difference may always be relevance. Teach Shakespeare through his interpreters. Show what each generation had to twist him into seeming to mean. And then maybe the hippies in your class will discover what *they* want to twist him into. Maybe you'll even discover what *you* do!"

Ah, why had she had to say *that?* Rhoda was Rhoda again.

"I wouldn't presume to twist him into anything," he said coldly. "It's always been my thesis that one can't look at him directly. Shakespeare is like the sun. He requires dark glasses."

"Exactly. In your case, he requires Betterton. Very well, use Betterton. *Be* Betterton!"

Marvin did not want to talk anymore now because he did not want yet to acknowledge how much she had excited him. He could hardly wait to be alone, and as soon as he could decently break off he hurried to the solace of his library in the back of the house, which looked over the East River to the commercial temples of downtown Manhattan. Closing the door behind him he went to the alcove where he kept his Thomas Betterton collection and breathed with a faint, sweet relief, as he always did, even a dozen times a day, to see it intact. Ah, Rhoda was right. She had to be right! He had started Shakespeare through Betterton. It was Betterton who would see him through.

In the center of the alcove was an old drawing in a heavy gilt frame over which protruded a small lamp that he now turned on. It revealed the portrait of a handsome, fleshy, clean-shaven, aquiline-nosed, round-cheeked, thick-lipped man of middle years with round, expressive eyes and a high, curled peruke that fell to his shoulders. The bronze plate on the lower board of the frame read: THOMAS BETTERTON. *1635–1710.* BY SIR GODFREY KNELLER. On alternate shelves in the alcove, to balance the books, were engravings of the great actor as Hamlet, Brutus, Falstaff, Coriolanus, Antony; playbills showing casts; glass cases with precious relics: shoe buckles, costume jewelry, daggers, bits of armor, snuffboxes. A silver casket used in *The Merchant of Venice* housed the precious remnants of an early Desdemona's handkerchief. On the bookshelves were ranged the quartos of the plays as adapted for Betterton by Davenant and Ravenscroft, including the actor's own stage copy of *Julius Caesar.*

Seated in the alcove, his sanctum, Marvin put together, piece by piece, the beautiful plan suggested by Rhoda's idea. He would make a virtue out of what had been cried up as his worst defect. He had been accused of worshiping the priest rather than the

deity, of preferring the great interpreter to what was being interpreted. But it was precisely his error that would redeem him.
He would save his situation by putting a spotlight on it. He
would, as Rhoda said, be Betterton!

Marvin stood, on the first Monday of the fall semester, before
a diminished and inattentive class. He opened his lecture in a
high, penetrating tone that seemed to challenge dissent.

"There is nothing, surely, in the whole history of English literature about which scholars and critics are more agreed than
that the late seventeenth-century editions of Shakespeare by such
'refiners' as Davenant, Tate and Ravenscroft represent the very
pinnacle of Philistine audacity. Yet the fact must be faced that
the great actor who more than any other man saved and re-
vitalized the declining reputation of the Swan of Avon acted —
presumably by preference — in these versions. Thomas Betterton
was the first pilgrim to Stratford, the first investigator to dig out
the meager facts and legends of the poet's life. As a young man
he had been directed in *Hamlet* by Davenant — Davenant, who
had seen Joseph Taylor play the role; Taylor, who had been
coached by Shakespeare himself! For all the amendments, the
violations, the horrors of these tampered-with texts, we can still
reach back through them and touch Betterton's hand, and
through Betterton we almost touch the white feathers of the
Swan!"

Marvin paused and glared into the auditorium. If they would
ever heckle, they would do so now. Well, he would give them
time, all the time they wanted.

"It must be important how such a man felt and interpreted
Shakespeare. We know from Pepys and from Addison that Betterton on the boards was unforgettable. Colley Cibber records
that he never heard him recite a line of tragedy wherein the
judgment, the ear and the imagination were not fully satisfied.
In *Hamlet,* Betterton made the Ghost as terrible to the spectator

as to himself. When he first caught sight of Hamlet's father's spirit, he paused in mute amazement. Then, very softly and gradually, he raised his tone from a near-whisper to one of solemn trembling, but always controlled, always respectful:

"Angels and ministers of grace, defend us!
Be thou a spirit of health, or goblin damn'd,
Bring with thee airs from heaven, or blasts from hell,
Be thy intents wicked, or charitable,
Thou com'st in such a questionable shape
That I will speak to thee: I'll call thee Hamlet,
King, Father, Royal Dane: O, answer me!"

It was not until he had reached the "Royal Dane" that he recognized that the voice to which he had been listening was a voice other than his own. It had a rich, low, reverberating tone; it was saturated in emotion and the deepest awe. Marvin trembled all over, but it was a tremble of ecstatic pleasure, as if every part of his chest and stomach and loins were being slowly and somehow delectably pulled up and out of his skin, as if his body were being liberated in some incomprehensible fashion from itself with a strange, orgiastic thrill. And the voice, the mysterious, tremulous, commanding voice, continued to declaim the whole speech, only the first half of which Marvin had any sense of knowing by heart, placing its emphases quite otherwise than Marvin would have placed them, but in each instance making him feel that he had leapt unexpectedly, rather wildly into the air but had alit, happily, on a trapeze that some unseen hand had sent winging to him just in time for his reaching fingers. When the voice stopped and his own lips closed after the "What should we do?" there was a thunderstruck silence followed by a startled, scattered applause.

He held up his hand.

"We do not know how the Ghost was played in Betterton's

day, but it seems likely that it varied less from today's Ghosts than the other characters varied from their modern counterparts. Of course, there is a legend that in Shakespeare's day he played the part himself."

Here Marvin started, in his most sepulchral tone, the speech beginning "I am thy father's spirit," but with a sharp, almost agonizing deflation of his euphoria, he at once recognized his own voice. Sitting down suddenly, for his legs seemed to bend beneath him, he continued the lecture from his notes until, just toward the end of the period, an idea struck him, and he looked up at the class and almost shouted:

> "Haste me to know it, that I, with wings as swift
>   As meditation, or the thoughts of love,
>   May sweep to my revenge!"

It was the voice! Of course! It would come only for Hamlet!

Students crowded around his desk at the end of the period, but he could not even understand their questions. He stared at them, dazed.

"I'm sorry, I have an appointment. I can only make it if I rush!"

And rush he did. His rush carried him all the way to the downtown subway before he stopped to consider where he was going. He was so excited that he dared not think. He got off the car at Grand Central and walked rapidly to the place where he always went when he was in that part of town: the Seven Gables Book Shop. Its beautiful mustiness, its gleaming leather and dustiness, its shabby magnificence cut out the city, the century, the whole horrible contemporary world. Michael Papantonio, sharp, quizzical, half-smiling, gaunt, looked up with the air of a man who would be surprised if anything could still surprise him.

"Why, Marvin! I was just going to call you."

"You've got a Betterton?"

"That's right! It's the *Hamlet* ninth edition you were looking for. From Betterton's library. With the cast of characters showing his wife as Ophelia. Does your happy instinct tell you the price I want?"

"Only that it's more than I want to pay!"

They both laughed — Marvin a bit hysterically — as they concluded their bargain.

Rhoda was very still and attentive that night, when he told her, at dinner, of his day's experiences. Like many unimaginative, literal-minded persons she was fascinated by the occult. Marvin knew that she even consulted an astrologist about some of her law cases.

"Of course, you suppose it's Betterton himself who haunted you," she observed.

" 'Visited' is the word I should prefer. Who else? Isn't he the person who would most care about reassembling his scattered relics?"

"Possibly. But might it not also be the spirit of some humble book collector who couldn't afford a Betterton collection in his own lifetime? And who is now putting one together through you?"

Marvin reflected that this was a very sisterly reaction.

"How, then, would you explain the voice?"

"Maybe it's the spirit of some poor down-and-out actor who never had a chance to play Hamlet."

"If it amuses you to think so."

"It doesn't amuse me, Marvin. It doesn't amuse me at all. I'm not a bit sure that this 'visitation' is a good thing."

"Even if it brings back my students?"

"Even so. Why should you care about a few more beards in your classroom? You have a distinguished library, an assured income, an established reputation . . ."

"No reputation is established these days!"

"Then what good will it do you to create a new one? It's one thing when we try to get in touch with the spirit world. It's quite another matter when it tries to get in touch with us. Watch out, Marvin!"

Marvin felt his heart pounding again as it had pounded that morning in his classroom. For a sick minute he wondered if this could be fear. But then he felt once more the strange pushing upward in his chest that had been accompanied by such a curious exaltation. "Oh, Rhoda, can't you and I face a fact every now and then?" he cried. "We make a great deal of what we do — you of your law, I of my literature — but can't we still admit that we haven't done much *living*?"

Rhoda's brown face seemed to shrink to a small, obdurate tan plate. "Speak for yourself," she muttered. "I'm satisfied that I've done my share of living."

"Well, I'm not! And maybe this is just my chance — my miraculous last chance — to live a bit. Wouldn't it be a terrible thing to miss it?"

"Marvin," his sister said in a suddenly diffident tone, and then she paused. "You don't suppose that this might . . . well, that it might have something to do with your nervous troubles of last summer?"

He had been waiting for this, and he almost spat the quotation at her:

> "My pulse, as yours, doth temperately keep time,
> And makes as healthful music; it is not madness
> That I have uttered: bring me to the test,
> And I the matter will re-word; which madness
> Would gambol from."

He stopped, for the voice was not Hamlet's, not Betterton's, but his own. In something like panic he excused himself from the table, saying that he had a lecture to prepare, and shut himself in the library, sitting in the Betterton alcove for the rest of the evening. Whatever the precious spirit was, it could not be summoned. That was clear. It came when it wanted and only then.

In the following weeks Marvin learned, bit by bit, how to live with his ghostly visitor. Even expectation could be fatal to the wonderful process of the latter's realization within the form of Marvin Lesterhouse. If he started to quote from a plan and listened for the great voice, he was sure to be disappointed. He had first to clear his mind — insofar as he was able — of all greedy anticipation. He would then relax his muscles, close his eyes, harken for his own voice and start. And then — at least sometimes — the great thing would happen. Of course, when he read non-Betterton roles, he did not expect anything to happen, and nothing for some weeks did, until one day, when he was reading the lines of Lucius to Brutus in the last act of *Julius Caesar,* the great voice suddenly sounded, but oddly shrill and piping and very far away. Marvin clenched his fists in a thrill of excitement as he speculated that this might have been a role that Betterton had played as a boy!

Word spread rapidly through the college that Mr. Lesterhouse had developed an extraordinary gift of aping ancient dramatic styles, and Marvin found that he sometimes had as many as fifty auditors in his class. Furthermore, the course was oversubscribed for the following semester, and the head of the English department called him to his office for congratulations.

"I don't know whether you noticed me, Marvin, in the back of your classroom the other day. You were lecturing on the different versions of *King Lear* from Tate to Pope. But when you recited from the heath scene — well, man, I've never heard anything like it! Where did you ever learn to do that?"

Marvin simply smiled demurely, as he always now did in answer to this question, and said nothing.

"Of course, I don't know to what degree the thing's authentic, but I don't care. We have such a devil of a time today interesting students in anything but civil rights and pollution that I wonder if your little performance — or whatever you call it — isn't just the kind of spark we need. Damn it all, even if it isn't the seventeenth century, maybe it is if they think it is!"

As Marvin rose now to leave, his smile was almost condescending.

"Oh, it's the seventeenth century, all right," he assured his superior.

He was happy, happy, he was sure now, for the first time in his life. All of the principal facts of his emotional biography — the sad, ailing, complaining, invalid mother; the petulant, terrifying father; the evasions of his long, scared boyhood; his sick envy of the strong, the beautiful, the loved — all this sorry heap of nonliving paled to nothing against the exploding orgasm of being Lear in the storm or Hamlet on the ramparts or Othello moving grimly, step by soft step, to his wife's chamber. Waking at night and remembering the great moments of the previous morning's class, he would find his eyes streaming with tears, happy tears, at the release, the heaven, the very *loving* of it.

If Rhoda eyed him strangely across the breakfast table, it no longer irritated him. He simply felt sorry for her, and he had no further inclination to make her understand that he *did* feel sorry for her. Rhoda's life seemed unbearably bleak to him now, and he trembled at the idea that she should ever see it as he saw it. He understood that he did, after all, care for her, that under the sibling tolerance that had been taken for granted between them there existed another, more substantial feeling created out of pity: pity for Rhoda's methodicalness, her exactitude, her high conscientiousness, her fairness; or rather, pity for the empty heart that these things had to fill. He tried to take more interest in her law practice, in her lame ducks at Legal Aid, but she tended to become grumpy at this, and he desisted, fearing that she might suspect the real reason for his sudden curiosity.

The beneficent spirit, in the meantime, did not limit its visitations to Marvin's classroom. It seemed dedicated to assist and illuminate him, not only as a professor and book collector but in other, anomalous capacities. One afternoon, sitting in the back of a taxicab on his way to his college library to chide the librarian for failing to bid high enough for an early Massachusetts prayer-book at a Parke-Bernet auction, he had a sudden, curious sense that the errand on which he was bound was a futile one. What on earth was the point of going so far uptown to see Mr. Kelper when at that very moment Mr. Kelper was indisposed for conversation? And why was he indisposed? The answer came in the vision that superimposed itself on that of the tumbled gray winter water of the Hudson that he could see from the West Side Drive. Mr. Kelper was indisposed because he was lying on the floor of the stackroom, his eyes closed and his chin covered with blood. Marvin leaned forward to speak to the taxi driver.

"I've changed my mind. Please get off the Drive at the next exit and take me back to Forty-second Street."

As the cab continued to move north, he felt something that grew rapidly from surprise to consternation at what he had done. Why, on the basis of this inexplicable vision, should he alter his destination? And wasn't it even more curious — so that now for the first time his heart took a quicker beat — that there should have been nothing in the vision that was scaring or even in the least unsettling? He had the oddest intuition, against all dictates of reason, that the bleeding Mr. Kelper was all right. The only thing that seemed to be all wrong was his own indulgence in an expensive cab ride to speak to a man who was in no position to be spoken to. Marvin shook himself, as if to shake off the whole absurd situation, and again leaned forward to speak to the driver.

"I'm sorry. I've changed my mind again. Let's go on to the college."

At the library the girl at the main desk informed him that Mr. Kelper could not see him. He had fainted from the close air in the stackroom, and his fall had caused a nosebleed. He had recovered, but had gone home to rest.

When Marvin told Rhoda about his experience that night before dinner, she stared at him in dismay.

"Then it's happened," she said gravely.

"What's happened?"

"What I was afraid of. That you would have a visitation that has nothing to do with Betterton. That has nothing to do with the seventeenth century. That has nothing, in fact, to do with anything you're interested in."

"Of course, the experience was entirely a subjective one," he explained hastily, as if to plead against the seriousness with which she took the little episode. Looking into her apprehensive eyes he felt some of the uneasiness that he had felt as a child when his mother had spied some glittering mechanical toy, given by a too indulgent uncle or aunt, that might have to be removed as "dangerous." "I could produce the cab driver to confirm my change of direction, but what would that prove?"

"Nothing." Rhoda's face was drawn. "But it doesn't matter. I believe you. I believe you absolutely."

"Shouldn't a lawyer be more skeptical?"

She shook her head. "A lawyer must know when to distinguish. There's always the borderline. When the normal slips over into the sinister."

Looking hard at his sister's pursed lips, Marvin had a sense of bafflement that he identified with the felt prohibition, going back to the dawn of all sensation, that had always seemed to fall across anything that was fun. It was the interdict against thumb-sucking, against sweets between meals, against daydreaming in the classroom and movies in the afternoon, against horrid little friends and the furtive manipulation of secret parts of the body. He could see his father's long pointing finger, indicating the alternative of violent ball games on concrete playgrounds, of standing up with one's back to a wall, straight, straight, straight up.

"Why sinister?" he demanded.

"Because you're being led on. Led on to something frightful. Oh, my dear Marvin, don't you see it?"

"I'm not your dear Marvin," he retorted. "Why do you call me that, all of a sudden? You've never called me that before."

"I know we're not a demonstrative pair, but we can still care about each other, can't we? Whom else have we got, I'd like to know? Oh, you have Betterton, you think, but that's just the point. Have you? Is it really Betterton who's doing this to you?"

"I know. You think it's some drunken ham actor who died in a ditch."

"Or worse. Much worse."

"Some devil, I suppose." There. *He* had been the one to say it, anyway.

"Something that's leading you on to do something horrible. Something that's tempting you. By giving you success with your students. Success with your book collecting. And now it's starting to show you the price. It's breaking you in gradually. With a first faint whiff of blood!"

Marvin shuddered. Never would he have dreamed that Rhoda could be so insinuating. But then he jumped up with a sudden, unexpected start of hope and walked quickly away from her. At the end of the room he whirled about to face her. But no. She was still the same Rhoda. The wild idea that the spirit of Mrs. Siddons had entered into *her* to play Lady Macbeth vanished. They were alone with fear. Discouragement gushed into his heart in a plunging, stunning flood.

"What a ridiculous idea," he muttered, but he covered his face with his hands and moaned aloud.

* * *

At a small stag dinner of bibliophiles in the Sutton Place home of Luke Reston, greatest of collectors, the tall, rangy, gray, smooth-voiced host was addressing his guests over the brandy glasses.

"I know everyone here has heard the gossip about Marvin Lesterhouse's helpful spirit. Now wait, Marvin, don't sputter till you hear what I have to say. It's to your advantage, I promise. I have recently acquired Thomas Betterton's own copy of the first volume of Rowe's 1709 Shakespeare, with the famous biographical introduction that, of course, refers to the great actor and his trips to Stratford . . ."

"Where on earth did you get *that*?"

"I thought that might arouse you, Marvin. You want to know how it slipped past *you*? Well, it turned up, uncatalogued, in the library of the Bishop of Earns which I bought last spring in Edinburgh . . ."

"Where is it? Can I see it?"

"You can have it. With my compliments. But I want to see if you can find it first. It's in the library, on a shelf. Suppose you go in there and bring it out. What would be a fair time to give you?" As Reston paused, the silence around the table became suddenly tense. It was broken when the host continued, with his best smile. "Or rather, how much time would it be respectful to exact of the beneficent spirit?" He pulled a watch from the pocket of his vest. "Shall we say ten minutes? It doesn't really matter. It would be impossible to find it unless one had luck — or guidance."

Marvin felt the close scrutiny of the table upon him. Everything in him seemed to be in suspense, in void. He could see

nothing but the fantastic treasure, in dull brown calf, that Reston
had dangled before his covetous mind's eye. He had not even
known that Betterton had seen the great edition, published just
before his death! When he had promised Rhoda to abandon his
dangerous game, he had never visualized such a temptation.

"You can time me," he heard himself say, "from the moment
I close the library doors."

Stepping into the big, dim, alcoved chamber beyond the dining
room, he shut the double doors behind him. Around him, above
him, before him, were shelves upon shelves of leatherbound volumes of every size and variety, some black or brown, some mag-
nificently gilded, some splendidly boxed, some protected by glass
panes. The walls and projecting cases were lined from floor to
ceiling with books. There was no relief but two French windows
looking out over the moonlit East River and the lighted portrait,
over the mantel, of a quaintly piratical-looking character with
pearls in his ears who was believed by some scholars to be Shakespeare himself, painted from life.

It may have been the unexpected character of the supposed
bard, with its bizarre suggestion of corsair activities, that made
Marvin again think of blood. For a few seconds he stood stark
still, transfixed with his fear. Then, for several precious minutes,
he hurried from alcove to alcove, trying desperately to make out
the plan of the library. As Reston had said, it was impossible.
Reston had arranged his books, as did many collectors, according
to a personal scheme. Marvin recalled the size of the Rowe
Shakespeare and tried to pick it out by walking past the shelves,
scanning them for dimensions. This, too, was futile. There were
hundreds of books of that same approximate size. In a minute,
the time would be up. Reston was right. He would never find
it without guidance.

He walked back to the center of the room and stood there,
his eyes closed, relaxing the muscles in his arms and stomach,

stripping his mind of everything but the picture of the title page of the first volume of Rowe. Then he shuddered in a strange ecstasy of terror as the familiar feeling crept over him, and he felt his feet moving, and his right hand rising to touch a brown volume in the middle of a brown shelf. He opened it to the title page that corresponded to the one impressed upon his mind.

He closed the book again and clutched it to his heart, sobbing suddenly, as he visualized Rhoda's pale, warning face.

"I'm sorry!" he cried aloud. "I can't!"

He replaced the book on the shelf and returned to the center of the room just as the double doors opened and Reston appeared, the curious faces of the others crowding behind him.

"Maybe it's the spirit's night off," Reston said in a kindly tone, when he saw that his guest was empty-handed.

Marvin simply shook his head, and then his host noticed his tear-stained eyes.

"I say, old man, you do take it hard!" he exclaimed. He turned to the others and waved them back. Then he closed the doors quickly and hurried to the shelf that Marvin had just visited to pluck forth the little volume.

"Please forgive the atrocious bad taste of the whole wretched incident," he begged as he handed it to Marvin. "Of course I meant to give it to you anyway. If you'll do me the honor of accepting it, it will help me to believe that you have not too much resented what has happened tonight."

But Marvin pushed the treasured gift away. "I'm not worthy of it!" he groaned. "I'm not worthy of *him.*"

And then, to the anguished embarrassment of his genial host, he fell on his knees, there on the carpet in the middle of the library, and sobbed with the abandonment of a despairing child.

Equitable Awards

GWENDOLEN BURRILL SAT facing her lawyer across a broad desk, the very bareness of which, except for an unspotted green blotter and a black pen stand that was obviously never used, suggested that its occupant, in the business of offering simply a brain full of ideas, operated more efficiently without encumbrance. But the stripped neatness of the desk, matched with the bleakness of the chamber, chaste except for a large, dull print of Bowling Green in the 1840s, depressed Gwen, making her feel that her own rather faded attributes — curly chestnut hair streaked with gray, skin more smooth than pink, a decayed girlishness that showed its forty-six years — were being harshly exposed, laid out, so to speak, one by one, on a long board, to be picked up appraisingly and then, presumably, put down again.

"Let me explain how the nineteen eighty divorce law works, Mrs. Burrill. It is based on the theory that marriage is a kind of business partnership. The court will assess the value of what you as a wife have contributed to this partnership and award you accordingly. And the division will encompass not only income but principal. In your case I'd go so far as to suggest that we're justified in asking for a fifty-fifty split right across the board. Half of your husband's total wealth, and, of course, a full half of his earned income until your death or remarriage."

"But how," Gwen protested, "can you argue that I contrib-

---

uted to his success in his law firm? He's slaved away there, day and night, for the last twenty years! Just the way you all probably do here."

"And how could he have done that if you hadn't been doing your part? Mr. Burrill has been able to give himself totally to his profession only because you have lifted the weight of his private life off his hands. Who looked after the home, the children, the vacations, the entertainments? Who freed him of all his petty cares, even his major ones? Why, Mrs. Burrill, I'll bet you even bought his shirts!"

"It's true. I did."

"And now that you've given him half your life, now that you've lost your chance for a professional career in which you might have done at least as well as he, are we to let him cast you aside like an old shoe? Excuse the expression! I'm afraid I got carried away."

Gwen smiled as sweetly as she was able, but it was less to spare the lawyer's feelings than to hide her own pain. Old shoe! But, of course, wasn't that just how this young woman *would* regard her? Miriam Storrs, juris doctor, couldn't have been more than thirty, probably less, and she had none of the semimasculine, tailored firmness that women of Gwen's mother's generation (and some of Gwen's) liked to associate with their career-oriented sisters, smugly deeming it the price they had to pay for their success in a man's world. But Miriam Storrs was blonde and even possessed of rather baby-blue eyes, and the fineness of her figure was only too apparent under that silly white dress with the flowered hem.

"Excuse me for asking a personal question, Miss Storrs. Are you married?"

"Oh, yes. My husband's a doctor. A pediatrician."

"And do you have children?"

"Not yet, but we hope to."

Gwen sighed. What a useless, idle creature she must seem to such a couple! A life wholly dedicated to domesticity — and a domesticity that had come to this!

"Do you like divorce work?"

"A case like yours, yes."

"Because you consider me a victim of male chauvinism?"

"Not really." Miriam's demeanor of bright professional sympathy faded a bit, and Gwen had a sudden glimpse of how her counselor might look to an adversary in court. "I assume you chose your own life and chose it freely. But you gave up certain opportunities when you did so, and your husband accepted that sacrifice. He shouldn't be allowed now to renege on his part of that implied contract. He must make you whole."

"How can that be done?" Gwen shrugged sadly as she rose to go. "But, of course, you mean only to the extent possible. Very well, I'm in your hands. I leave it all to you."

Gwen walked home that fine spring day all the way from Miriam Storr's office on Madison Avenue and Fiftieth Street to her own apartment on Eighty-sixth. Her life had been largely spent in the blocks that she traversed. Her parents still lived in the brownstone in which she had been raised on Sixty-ninth Street.

Passing that street, she almost turned back to call on them. But no, she decided, it was better to be alone. Their sympathy was always excessive, a bit unsettling, and then they had never really cared for Sidney, never thought him good enough for her. Oh, they had been decent to him, of course, and had recognized that he was bright and industrious and would get ahead, but they had hoped . . . well, that if she *had* to marry a lawyer, it would be one who, when he had made his name and partnership, would go on into government, or diplomacy, or some sort of higher education. But Sidney, with that pale skin, that dark, faintly unshaven look, those staring red-lined eyes that seemed to search for a problem and a solution in the simplest things, with his way of losing himself and the world in work, could never break away, or perhaps even want to break away, from those cool, aggrandizing clients who were shrewd enough to know, without ever being big enough to tell him, how indispensable a tool he was to their daily machinations.

She had not suspected his almost compulsive habits of work before they were married. She knew that he labored hard, but then so did all the other young lawyers among her new, post-college friends. She considered that she labored fairly hard herself. She was a secretary in a publishing house and shared an apartment with her former Vassar roommate. The novel sense of liberty from her parents, though they lived only a few blocks away, was intoxicating, and she dined with them once a week to tell them just how intoxicating it was.

"Hardly any of my group were brought up in New York," she told her mother proudly. "They don't seem to be shackled to the past the way I was. They haven't so many appendages. They're free!"

"And what is Mr. Burrill free of?" Her mother had already divined the growing intimacy between Gwen and the young lawyer.

"Why, free of everything! Except, of course, of the law. And, perhaps, a little of me now." Gwen giggled, rather smugly.

"Does he have no family?"

"Oh, he has a mother, I think, in Milwaukee. And a brother someplace else. But his father deserted them years ago. They don't even know where he is."

"How desirable!" Gwen's mother exchanged a smile with her husband.

"Oh, Daddy, I didn't mean . . ."

"Of course, you didn't, dear."

Sidney seemed to have inherited a brain from nowhere and

to be quite willing to place it a hundred percent at the service of his employers. He never looked beyond his firm; he never questioned its right to use every bit of Sidney Burrill for its general purposes. He was like a faithful hound that needed but a single master, and that would probably be just as content with a second if anything should happen to the first. But the very exclusiveness of this loyalty created in him an oddly attractive independence about other things. Sidney was, as Gwen boasted, a free soul — outside his firm. He had no prejudices, no boredoms, no tiresome idiosyncrasies. He was gay and easy with people at parties; he liked to drink and, as she soon discovered, to make love. She had no doubt, when he first became serious about her, that she would be to his heart what his law firm was to his mind. But it had not taken many months of marriage to teach her that if she had his love, his time belonged to others. And the years simply confirmed this.

She remembered thinking that things would be different when Sidney attained his ambition and became a partner in his firm. Then he would take more time off, and they would do things together. But her father had warned her against this illusion.

"Lawyers and businessmen in Sidney's league can't afford to slacken the pace," he had told her, rather complacently, as it now struck her. "They might make the unpleasant discovery that they had prepared themselves for nothing else in life."

Implicit in her parents' view of Sidney was the attitude that he might as well work his silly head off as spend his leisure time boring them, and presumably boring Gwen. But it simply wasn't true that Sidney bored her. When he wasn't working, he could be charming: affable, amiable, open-minded, funny and interested in all the little things that were going on around him. In the country he loved to identify birds and flowers and to take the boys on long walks. The intensity that he brought to his law

practice was also available for the mixing of a cocktail, the solution of a crossword puzzle, or the fixing of defective plumbing.
The trouble with these periods of relaxation was only their brief-
ness. Sidney by Sunday afternoon was already restlessly looking
forward to Monday morning. He was a pale Faust, with glittering eyes, who had been released only for a day.

He was perfectly aware of the problem that his industry posed
for her, and perfectly frank in the remedy that he always put
forward.

"You should get a job. You've much too good a mind to waste
it all day."

"You call it wasted at home?"

"To the extent it's not needed, yes."

It was in vain that she argued that little Sidney, who suffered
from asthma, needed constant maternal attention, and that Fred,
with dyslexia, had to be helped with all his homework. Sidney
simply countered with an offer to engage a nurse and tutor. This
outraged Gwen's mother, who told her that he had no sensitivity
about the needs of children and who accused him of wanting to
convert his whole family into money-making machines. Eventu-
ally a solution for Gwen's daytime problem was found by her
father, who procured her a part-time, mildly paying job in a
small family foundation, processing applications for scholarships.
Sidney said nothing against this, but his failure ever to ask her
a question about what she was doing at her office was sufficient
evidence of what he was thinking. Work to him was a sacred
concept. It should never be faked.

As she walked on north now Gwen made herself speculate on
the harm that her parents might have done to her marriage.
Certainly they had been overprotective. They had shielded her
from reality. Yet she could imagine the defenses they would make
to such an indictment. Had they not always tried to be reasonable, civilized? What rational human being could have seriously

questioned their standards? Had her father not sagely used a comfortable inheritance to make himself an authority in political science? Was not her mother an active member of *two* hospital boards? Where could she fault the way they had combined the decorative life with the useful one, high ideals with sound common sense, the dues to Caesar and the dues to God?

And yet. She recalled now a dinner party that she and Sidney had given for Simon Blunt, the man who had put together the lots in lower Manhattan for New Orange Plaza. She remembered her father's jovial air with Blunt's friends and the sudden change in his tone when, standing by her out of hearing of the others, he had whispered sharply: "I hate to see you in this nest of pirates!"

When she had had the indiscretion to relate this to Sidney after the party, he had exploded.

"I think your old man has one hell of a nerve to slam people who make a go of it in fields that he was too dainty to put a toe in! How the hell does he think the money was made that lets him sit on his ass and write beautiful prose about wicked governments? And it isn't even as if he had enough to make you independent of me! By the time he kicks the bucket and Uncle Sam has taken his cut, you may be thanking your lucky stars for your grubbing husband. You may even learn to be a little more friendly to a man like Blunt."

"Do you imply that I wasn't friendly to him tonight?"

"Oh, you were perfectly correct. The great lady of the Colony Club. But if he'd seen the way you are with your own friends, he'd have got the idea fast enough! That's why I'm so careful never to mix my clients with your crowd."

Gwen had reflected that she had never noticed this. "You had Mummie and Daddy tonight."

"Only because you insisted. You thought it might 'amuse' them. Don't worry. I won't make that mistake again."

"Daddy simply can't understand why you have to work for people like that. Nor can I. Mr. Blunt *is* a pirate, isn't he? Everyone says so."

Sidney had turned away in disgust. "Let's just put it that I like the Jolly Roger!"

When Gwen got back to her apartment, empty now with the two boys in college, and had mixed herself a solitary cocktail, she found herself wondering if her parents might not have made a mistake by inculcating in the future wife of a real-estate lawyer such moral fastidiousness. But what had she wanted? she could hear her father indignantly demanding. An amoral education? With Machiavelli as a preceptor? She shook her head. No. But perhaps she should have been taught a little more respect for the men who had to make the money. The trouble might have been that she had been brought up to be unworldly without being wholly unworldly, and that she had not been one of those able to work out the necessary compromise. Her brother, Fred, had no problem; he was naturally vulgar. He would have been at home with Sidney's toughest client. And her sister, Phoebe, was naturally pure; she was perfectly happy spending her days as a therapist in a home for retarded children. But Gwen now faced the fact that she had been neither a worldling nor an anchorite. She had always taken for granted that she would be privileged to drink the clear waters of the spring of idealism and at the same time profit from the golden calf, without muddying the former or worshiping the latter. And she had had the nerve to look down on Sidney!

The next morning found her back in the office of the still-patient Miriam Storrs. But the latter's smile was just a trifle mechanical.

"I had to tell you something!" Gwen started right off. "All last night, I kept thinking of what you'd said about how I'd contributed to Sidney's career. About my looking after the children and entertaining for him. But it's not true! We could have afforded a nurse, and both boys went off to boarding school when they were fourteen. And as for entertaining, I was never warm and cozy with Sidney's clients the way I was with my own friends."

"I'm sure they never noticed the difference."

"No, but Sidney did. He resented it terribly!"

Miriam seemed not quite to know how to take this. "Still, you went through with the parties and you raised the children. I suggest, Mrs. Burrill, that we confine ourselves to the facts and not to your private guilt complexes. Your husband accepted the role that you chose to play. As we say in the law, you relied on him to your detriment. *That* is the basis of our demands."

Gwen hesitated now, staring at the floor, before saying what she knew she had to say. Suddenly she raised her head and stuck her chin forward. "There's something else. I had an affair."

Miriam looked surprised. She took off her glasses and pushed her chair back. "Tell me about it."

"It was two years ago. In Paris. An appropriate place, you will say. But I hadn't thought Paris would bring me anything like that. Sidney's firm had decided he was too specialized for a man who might one day become a top partner. So they sent him abroad for a year to run the French office. I had thought it would be simply bliss. He and I could start all over again! I would have a real function in his life at last. In France a woman has a much greater role in her husband's business. And I could *help* Sidney. I spoke French and he didn't, and I'd been an art history major as Vassar."

"And it didn't turn out that way?" Miriam's little smile of sympathy was almost condescending.

"It didn't." Gwen rose to turn away from her lawyer, ashamed of her own sudden tears. "The children were at school in New England. I had no friends in Paris, no family, not even my silly old foundation to play with. I had nothing under the sun to do. And Sidney worked all day and night, just as he had in New York!"

"There were no clients to entertain?"

"Oh, some. But mostly Americans. And partners from his firm who happened to be traveling abroad. With their ghastly wives. We might as well have stayed in New York, for all the change it made in Sidney's life. We joined a tennis club in Neuilly, and I began to take lessons there in the mornings with the pro. He seemed a nice young man, actually not French — he was Swiss — and . . ."

"He was the guy?"

"He was the guy."

*   *   *

Alain came only twice to the apartment on the rue Murillo, both times at noon. On the tennis court he had been gentle, doe-eyed, almost servilely polite. It had seemed nothing less than a miracle to her that those dark, watery eyes, those thin lips, half-spread in a self-deprecating smile, should have suddenly expressed an apologetic but still articulate desire. And a desire for her, a matron who might have been, if not his mother, at least a young aunt! To have rejected his proposal that he call at the apartment some morning in the absence of "Monsieur" would have seemed like spitting in the eye of a fate that was at last offering her a chance to "live"!

When he came, however, he left behind him any seeming awareness of social inferiority. His manners were still correct, but he did not linger about his business. It was evident that she was nothing to him but a frustrated, middle-aged American female, still just attractive enough to provide a brief satisfaction. There was no need to dally, to talk, to pretend. The very way he tied his tie, carefully adjusting the knot as he complacently regarded his image in Sidney's shaving mirror, showed her that she was already forgotten. When he left after the second visit, it was perfectly apparent that he was not going to come again.

Indeed, there would have been no drama at all had not Sidney, coming home in the middle of the day with an inflamed sore throat, passed Alain in the hall lobby.

"I saw your little frog tennis pro downstairs," he said when he came in. "He wasn't coming here, was he?"

"You can't call him a little frog!" she heard herself suddenly cry. "He's my lover!"

And then she collapsed on the sofa, beating the cushions with both hands, giving rein to sudden hysterical sobs, screaming that she was nothing but a tramp, shouting at him to cast her off, to divorce her, to take the boys, and finally announcing that she wanted to die!

And what did *he* do? He sat down beside her; he took her hands in his; he pleaded with her; he consoled her; he blamed himself. And finally he took her in his arms and made love to her with a passion that he had not shown since their honeymoon.

* * *

Miriam's voice rose sharply. "He condoned the adultery?"

"You mean, slept with me, knowing what I'd done?"

"Yes. Didn't he?"

"He did."

"Then he's lost all ground for complaint."

Gwen turned almost angrily on her counselor. "I think your law's disgusting! Because he was decent enough to overlook it, his case goes out the window?"

"Isn't that where he should have wanted it to go when he resumed marital relations?"

Gwen could think of nothing to say to this. "I thought I had to tell you, anyway," she murmured ruefully.

"It's quite all right, Mrs. Burrill. I'm glad you did."

"Won't you please call me Gwen?"

"Gwen."

Her walk home was filled with bitter memories. Perhaps things would have been all right had they only stayed in Paris. Perhaps that "second honeymoon" would have lasted. But the sudden death of the managing partner of Sidney's firm, followed by Sidney's own elevation to that position, had brought about not only their precipitate return to New York, but the replunging of Sidney, even more deeply, if possible, into his old routine.

And there was a new difference now, an invidious one. Sidney was no longer allowed to devote himself wholly to the demands of his clients: he had to handle the administrative work. It was his new task to grapple with the business machines that had revolutionized office life in the seventies, and in particular with a computer that cast a hard yellow beam into every corner of the firm, showing precisely how much and how little each partner and associate contributed to the general income, and exposing wasted hours and padded time sheets. Sidney rapidly became not only an expert but an enthusiast in this new system, and when he came home at night, he would tell Gwen, with what she considered a rather unpleasant satisfaction, what "dead wood" he had been able to lop off that day. The dead wood, unhappily, was apt to be made up of men and women.

It did not take Sidney long to carry his computer methods into the home. What was Gwen, or their apartment, or even the fine silver service her parents had given her for a wedding present, really contributing to the firm? The new Sidney was inclined to drop comments about what a "superb job" this or that wife of a partner was doing in the matter of amusing and taking about the town visiting clients and their families.

"But I wonder what good that kind of thing really does," she protested at last. "Don't clients really come to you for your expertise in the law? You're not in the entertainment business, are you?"

"No, but there's no point kidding ourselves that the kind of expertise we offer is unique. Between two equal experts the prospective client will pick the one with the most fringe benefits."

"And that's what I am? A fringe benefit?"

"No, it's what you *could* be. Take Dottie Somers. She had Mrs. Knox, the wife of the president of Ellis Petrol, in tow all last week. She took her to two musicals, the opera, a bicycle race in Central Park and to see the baby polar bear in the Bronx Zoo."

"But, Sidney, if I did that kind of thing all day, I'd have no life left of my own!"

"What sort of a life do you have now?"

She had little to answer to this, but her very soul revolted at the idea of emulating Dottie Somers and pandering to a lot of pushing, arrogant spouses of corporate executives, who would surely take her as much for granted as any other company facility. Her mother and grandmother had never had to do that sort of thing! Her father and his father would never have asked it of them. They were gentlemen, after all, who respected their wives. Could one imagine her mother being smooth, flattering, compliant? Could one conceive of her murmuring, in the liquid tones of the odious Dottie Somers, "Now, Mrs. Knox, I'm going to show you what is simply the darlingest thing in all of our five boroughs, the cuddliest, jolliest, most beguiling bearlet you ever saw in all your born days!"

"I suppose I could do it," she said gloomily, "if that's what you really want of me."

"I don't! You can't do that sort of thing properly unless you like it. And I'm not such an ass as to kid myself you're ever going to like it."

But this seeming acceptance of her as he deemed her hopelessly to be was far from philosophic. It was informed with a deepening resentment. In the following year the brief moment of their Paris reconciliation faded until it seemed at last as unreal as her memory of the French capital, a lost paradise of soft golden light where people talked, unaccountably, of everything in the world but business machines. Under the darker American sky, in the thinner American air, her old adultery, however brief, however unimaginable, began to take on a scarlet hue. She was sure that Sidney brooded over it. Had he not forgiven her too abruptly? Had that affair with the fatuously grinning tennis pro really been the product of a fleeting moment of despair and abandon? Or had it been rather the affirmation of her longstanding marital disloyalty, the supreme expression of her repudiation of all her husband's values?

When she found the courage at last to ask Sidney if he were not regretting his magnanimity, his answer precipitated the first unhealable crack in their relationship.

"On the contrary, I look back upon my behavior in Paris as simply childish. Anytime you want another tennis pro, please feel at liberty. We have reached the point, you and I, where neither should reproach the other for such a simple diversion."

She stared at him in mute amazement. So that was how it came! "Meaning that you already have one?" she gasped.

"Meaning no such thing," he retorted briskly. "But meaning that I consider myself perfectly entitled to. Can you deny it?"

After this tart interchange what was left of their marriage fell rapidly apart. Sidney slept in the boys' bedroom and rarely came home for dinner. Finally, after an extensive business trip to the West Coast, he moved to a hotel directly on his return and wrote her that he would be staying there indefinitely. Yet when he was called by Miriam Storrs, he was outraged.

"Who the hell is this female you've sicked on me?" he demanded on the telephone.

"Miss Storrs? She's my lawyer. Daddy got her for me. Do you suggest I don't need one?"

"Certainly I do! We can handle this thing ourselves. Why pay lawyers?"

"I'm sure you won't have to pay yours."

"But there's no issue between us. I'm quite prepared to be adequately generous."

"I call that begging the question."

"Damn it all, Gwen, you don't have to fleece me!"

"I'm going to hang up now, Sidney. It's not ethical for you to try to bypass my lawyer."

At this Sidney's language became obscene, and she did hang up.

* * *

A week after Miriam had submitted to Sidney a first draft of the separation agreement, she summoned Gwen to her office.

"Of course your husband has rejected everything we proposed. That was to be expected at this stage. But he has done something I didn't expect."

"And what is that?"

"Well, he's not quite the male chauvinist I'd thought. Like you, he's retained a woman lawyer."

"Really? Who?"

"Hester Pearson. She's an associate in his office. Attractive. And bright, too. She was in my class in Columbia Law."

"Will it make any difference? I mean, her representing Sidney? Will it make him any tougher to deal with?"

"We'll soon see. They're here. Both of them. Waiting in the conference room. They want to talk to us."

"But why?" Gwen asked in dismay. "How can that possibly help?"

"They think there's something to be gained by talking this out."

Gwen assented at last, reluctantly, and Miriam got up to lead her down the corridor to a closed door. Opening it, she revealed Sidney and his lawyer seated together at the end of a long table. Miss Pearson had a calm, square, immobile face with eyes that gazed steadily at the object of her attention, which was at the moment very much Gwen. Her brown hair, neatly waved, was parted in the middle. She did not rise, but received her visitors as if they had been clients in her own office. Sidney looked steadfastly out the window after simply nodding to his wife. Embarrassed in this conclave of females, he was evidently planning to say as little as possible.

"What is the purpose of this bizarre confrontation, Miss Pearson?" Gwen demanded, a bit breathlessly, after she and Miriam were seated. Sidney's lawyer continued to contemplate her coolly before giving her answer.

"I should say at the outset, Mrs. Burrill, that your husband was opposed to this interview. But he has always spoken of your considerable intelligence, and that is what I am counting on. It seems to me that the four of us here should be able to work out an equitable solution to this domestic problem quite as well as any judge or jury."

"That's fine. All Sidney has to do is meet Miss Storrs's terms."

"But, you see, he is not going to do that. Rather than give up any portion of his principal, he will resist your demands all the way to the court of appeals. It is his position that you have made no substantial contribution to his success as a lawyer and that you are therefore entitled only to a reasonable share of his income."

Gwen contemplated curiously the grave, judicial countenance before her. "Do you really think, Miss Pearson, that your putting the matter that way makes it more attractive to me? Is that how you would try to persuade a jury?"

"I am not a litigator, Mrs. Burrill."

"I see. Perhaps that was a wise choice."

"Can it, will you, Gwen!" Sidney did not even turn from the window as he snapped this out.

"I think we should try to avoid personalities," Miriam suggested nervously. "They're always counterproductive."

Miss Pearson ignored everyone but Gwen. "Does it offend you that I appeal to your intellect, Mrs. Burrill? I suggest that we consider the facts. Your marriage has been a total failure. There has been infidelity on both sides, and there is no vestige left of mutual affection."

"And whose fault is *that*?" Gwen demanded angrily.

"Fault is a misleading term. Neither party contributed what was needed to sustain the marriage. You were not interested in your husband's work. His clients either bored or offended you. And he gave you no support in solving the problem of what to do with your own life."

"Oh, you see that, do you?"

"I see it very clearly. He expected you to look after yourself and let him work. And you allowed yourself to build your life on the expectation of what you and he would do with leisure time that he was never going to have. The situation was hopeless from the beginning."

"Let me say that it surprises me, knowing him as you do, that you should have wanted to take this case."

"Because I find it not only interesting but socially significant. You belong to what is probably the last generation of women who have tried to believe that, to them, the home could be all. And your husband belongs to what is probably the last generation of men who have tried to believe that, to them, the home could be nothing. I suggest that you would both do better to admit frankly the failures of the past and not use them as a source of personal profit or revenge."

"You mean I will be better able to face the future with *less* money?"

"Less than you are now asking for, yes. Not less than you need to support yourself appropriately. Mr. Burrill is not sticking at any particular figure. All that is perfectly adjustable. What I am arguing is that he should not be embittered by having to pay for a contribution to his career that he does not believe existed, and that you should not be falsely consoled by an unjust enrichment. For you, too, Mrs. Burrill, have a new life to put together. And I know it will be better for you to build it on a truth rather than a pretense!"

"Well, of all the bloody nerve!" Gwen turned wrathfully to her own lawyer. "I'm going home!" she cried. "I've had enough of this crap. But if you can think of anything tougher to demand, demand it!"

This time, on her way home, she did stop at her parents' and spent the afternoon with them, discussing the divorce and Sidney's abominable lawyer. They lavished upon her every consolation; they praised her and applauded her resolution. She rolled about in the tepid bath of their sympathy, rubbing the soapsuds of their endearments against her wounded ego. She listened hungrily to the base epithets that they heaped on Sidney. But she knew all the while, like the dull little ache somewhere deep within her of a fatal ailment, that it was all of no avail.

Back in her own apartment, she called Miriam, who was still in her office.

"She's right, that little bitch of a lawyer of Sidney's," she blurted out. "She's right, and you know it. I'm not entitled to anything more than what Sidney's giving me now. I could see it in your eyes that you thought so too!"

"I think we can suspend any discussion of what your lawyer does or does not think until you've had a chance to consider a new aspect of this case. It may render my attitude wholly irrelevant."

"What new aspect?"

"Something I've just been told. By a friend of mine who also works for your husband's firm. Can't you guess what it is?"

Gwen closed her eyes as she felt the quick hardening in her chest. "That girl is his . . . mistress?"

"And confidently expects to become the second Mrs. Burrill."

"But how can she want to?" Gwen cried in anguish. "After what she knows about him as a husband!"

"Oh, they won't need a home. They'll have two careers!"

For an hour after this call, Gwen paced up and down her living room, her mind a flaming battlefield. On one side, drawn up in neat, uniformly marching and wheeling platoons, were the small, gray, disciplined figures of reason, bearing their little banners with legends about getting on with life, not throwing good money after bad, cuttting one's losses, liquidating useless pasts. But around these stalwart stubbornly advancing soldiers ranged the ragged, amorphous battalions of self-pity, of jealousy, of hate, swarming over the forces of reason, blotting them out of sight, ripping up their standards with long bloody claws. "No, no, be miserable with us!" they seemed to wail. "Be miserable with us, and we will make everyone else miserable too!"

Why was their temptation so irresistible? Why was the black curtain that seemed to swoop down upon her so alluring? Why did she know so surely that it would be her fate?

She dialed Miriam's number again and found that industrious woman still at work. "I want to divorce Sidney for adultery!"

"You see, I was correct," the lawyer responded in what struck Gwen as a flat tone. "It *did* make a difference. But that's all right. I anticipated your call. I'm already working on your petition."

Still Life

I THOUGHT I HAD DONE WELL in choosing Peter Kip as the subject of my master's thesis for New York University Art School. He had been almost entirely neglected by art critics and historians since his death in 1960, and even in his lifetime his exquisite, semi-impressionistic studies of the rooms and gardens of his wealthy friends had united in cool disdain the devotees of the abstract and the propagandists of the left. But now that realism had returned to the art scene, I suspected that Kip might be due for a reappraisal, and I scanned the art page of my Sunday *Times* with nervous dread lest Hilton Kramer or John Russell should have anticipated my thesis, or some gallery should have mounted a retrospective show. It was not that I begrudged poor Kip any belated recognition that might come his way, but surely, being dead, he could wait one little year to give me the glory of being his herald!

I had another reason for selecting Kip, a more personal one. There were no people in his pictures. From his fortieth year to his death, at the age of sixty-five, he had never used a model or even a sitter. It was true that human figures were depicted, or at least suggested, in the tapestries and portraits and statues that adorned his painted chambers, but there were no living, breathing creatures, except as might be deduced from a pile of books on a bedtable, a door left ajar, a wheelbarrow standing by a flowerbed.

I liked this aspect of Kip's art because physically I had always been rather a shrimp, and one of my legs was half an inch shorter than the other. I indulged in the fantasy that my pallor and blondness, with the dubious aid of rather dirty blue eyes, made up in part for this, that there might be the embryo of a romantic angel within the shape of a cricket, but I was basically too much of a realist not to be aware that this was the crudest kind of sentimental compensation. I resented my better-equipped fellow students when they extolled art that emphasized bodily beauty and vigor and the delights of sex. Kip was not only a thesis but a potential creed.

The theory that I began with was that Kip was trying to express the personality of each room that he painted. But could a room be properly said to have a personality other than its expression of a human arrangement? I contended that it might. Studying the reproductions of these interiors in the privately printed testimonial volume on Peter Kip in N.Y.U.'s art library at the old James B. Duke house (itself a Kip room!), I developed the hypothesis that something might occupy a room when it was emptied of people, something evoked not necessarily by its owner, or even by events that had occurred in it, but simply by its becoming freed of human domination — something mute, passive, beyond affirmation or protest, perhaps even beyond resignation.

My thesis project was only grudgingly approved by my faculty adviser, Donald Cole. He did not consider Kip "important," an adjective that he tiresomely overused. Cole was one of those handsome, tweedy, pipe-smoking extroverts who should never have been in art at all, and who had only chosen teaching when he had failed as a painter. He condescended to all artists, living or dead, except Michelangelo, Leonardo and any abstract expressionist of the nineteen fifties or sixties. He would have been surprised had he known that I regarded him as a toady who would have thrown any of his gods to the wind at a single nod from Clement Greenberg. But I had to talk to him because he had actually known my subject when he had been a student in Paris, and what other observers were there within my reach who had penetrated the exalted social milieu of the Kips?

"Let me start by admitting that he was a perfect brick to me," my mentor expounded. "Why should he, already old, presumably set in his habits, with a beautiful château in Fontainebleau, go out of his way to be kind to a young Yankee artist without a cent and, as it turned out, without talent? But he did. On the strength of a simple note from a niece. He asked me out for a weekend, provided me with a horse and a gun, and introduced me to all sorts of important people. He even took me to Picasso's studio! But Kip wasn't what I had come to Paris for. His was not the place for an artist."

"Why not, if it was good enough for Picasso?"

"Oh, Picasso didn't go *there*. Mrs. Kip had no use for artists. She went in for the rich and fashionable. People like the Windsors."

"What was she like?"

"Querulous. A semi-invalid. Perhaps a bit of a *malade imaginaire*. Such a contrast to him, with his athletic build and almost lineless face! And she didn't even have a fortune. The money was all his. Nobody could figure out why he married her."

"Perhaps he felt sorry for her."

"Perhaps. But I have a different theory. When a handsome, eligible bachelor marries a poor, unattractive woman, without even the health to give him children, she must have some asset that doesn't meet the eye."

"And what was that?"

"Exactly. What? I kept trying to figure it out at Fontainebleau. Kip was too perfect not to be false. I made a game of watching him to see if I couldn't smoke him out. One morning he appeared in a hunting jacket so splendid that it seemed to give him away.

But no, on closer observation, the elbows showed just the right amount of wear. Then I thought I'd catch those wonderful manners slipping into unctuousness. But he had the guts to walk out of the smoking room while the local duc de Guermantes was telling an anti-Semitic story! And finally, when I decided I had him typed as a faddish collector of fashionable moderns, what did he do but show me a salon painting he'd just bought of a fat cardinal sipping wine? Oh, don't tell me he wasn't the most exquisite old fraud that ever breathed! He might have been John Gielgud playing the perfect gentleman. It was beautiful, but it was still an act."

Cole professed to enjoy candor from students, so I did not feel it necessary to hang on too tightly to my short string of temper.

"Are you sure you aren't showing academic prejudice? If a man plays a crack game of bridge and is a first-class shot, must he be worldly and superficial? What about Kip's war record? Didn't he spend three years in the trenches, first in the French army and then in ours? Didn't he get the Croix de Guerre? Or can't a man be a good artist and a hero?"

"I concede the war record. But a man can face Armageddon and still be afraid of a rat."

"And where is the rat in Kip's case?"

"I should say buried somewhere in the deep, inexhaustible mine of sex."

"Oh, always, of course," I retorted. "If a man's a gentleman, it's because he was in love with his grandmother. And if he acts like a saint to a poor invalid wife, he's making up for homosexual urges."

I had finally succeeded in irritating the placid Cole, who didn't like me much anyway. "Well, why not?" he demanded. "Isn't the invalid wife of a man as strikingly handsome as Kip his obvious defense, not only against predatory women, but against sex itself? I miss my bet if your plaster saint wasn't a frustrated pederast who hid inclinations that scared the hell out of him (hero though he was) behind an impregnable wall of marriage and outward masculinity. How else could he have found a woman who would keep off the girls (and boys) and ask for no disgusting bed work in return?"

So there it was, the inevitable, banal modern argument. I left Cole in disgust, but his idea horridly stayed with me. I had a photograph of Kip as a young man, taken in his atelier. I had thought it the charming portrait of an athlete turned artist, like James's hero in *The Tragic Muse,* fine, earnest, straightforward, dedicated, a gentle gentleman without pretensions or condescension. But now I found myself wondering if I could not make out in the steady gaze of the eyes, in the seeming stillness of the pose, a kind of holding back, a sense of self-preservation from life. It was incredible that such a man should have married an invalid. Unless he were a saint. Or unless . . .

I found myself constantly studying a large colored reproduction which I had pinned over my desk, of a Kip, depicting the landing of a grand stairway in some old Paris mansion. Most of the canvas was occupied by the stairway mural, inspired by David's *The Battle of the Romans and Sabines.* What struck me now was that the rushing, agitated women, some carrying babies to appeal to their consorts in case their own charms should be insufficient, seemed fussy, clumsy, unsexy. One wondered if they would succeed in stopping the warriors from proceeding with a battle that was really a kind of glorious sport to them. The dominating figure in the mural was a magnificent young man, totally and rashly nude, except for a helmet. He was standing, his legs apart, his back to the viewer, his fine Roman profile presented, one arm stretched back, about to hurl a spear. His brown muscular figure and buttocks were painted with an erotic feeling totally absent in the female figures. As in Michelangelo, only the male appealed.

With the glib Freudianism of our era, I now moved over to Cole's position. I drew this deduction: Kip, in indulging his love of the male figure, had to protect himself twice: he could approach the nude only in a picture in a picture. He could say, therefore, to his demon or conscience, or whatever it was that was bugging him, "But I was only painting what was there! Was it *my* fault if the room happened to contain a mural with a naked youth?"

And now, of course, I saw it all: the hopeless shame, to a man of his class and generation, of such unspeakable hidden lusts; the quest for a refuge in a world of forms; the restraint of all emotion, even bad temper, lest it betray; the ultimate creation of a world of beauty utterly independent of the flesh, a soft, static heaven of *fauteuils* and *bergères* that no human posteriors sat upon, and of gray paneled dining rooms, with French windows opening on fragrant gardens, where no gross jaws chewed. Yet the naked Roman warrior still broke in. Could I use this kind of evidence, if evidence it were, in my thesis?

And then, by a curious coincidence, I was confronted with a very different aspect of Kip's elusive personality. One of my courses was drawing, and my class had been working for a week with a famous old model known as Florence, who had posed for Frederick MacMonnies when he had sculpted his Central Park Arethusa, whose well-contoured backside, presented to a Lutheran church across the avenue, had caused a lively litigation. But there was no trace of that shapely figure in the huge, sagging, wrinkled old cow who sat for us now, totally stripped except for a floppy black hat with feathers. She was certainly a character, and if anything happened to annoy her, she would retort in a flowing billingsgate that delighted the class.

My drawing instructor told me during a coffee break that I should talk to Florence. "She modeled for that poshy expatriate you're specializing in, what's his name? The one who did all those fancy French boudoirs?''

"Peter Kip?" I asked in consternation. "But he painted in Paris!"

"Oh, Florence is an international tramp. She started in London. Then Paris. Finally New York. I know she looks like the Victorian monument, but things weren't always that way. In her time she's slept with half the painters in Europe. If she could only write, she could make a fortune with her memoirs. Maybe you could ghost them for her. She'd make a better thesis than old Kip anyway!"

"Do you suppose *he* slept with her?" I demanded, ignoring his slur on my subject.

"Ask her. She loves to yack about her past."

"You mean straight out? Just like that?"

"Well, take the old girl out for a drink at least. She's a real booze hound. Don't worry about getting her talking. It's getting her stopped that'll be your problem."

I was shy about approaching Florence, and the situation was not ameliorated by her immediate assumption that my intentions were carnal. I had to admire her self-assurance, considering that she could have been my grandmother! But when we were settled in a corner of a local bar — she with her undiluted bourbon, rouged, floppy-hatted, black-garbed, a crazy caricature of a Toulouse-Lautrec, and I with my Perrier, a mere chick to her massive hen (how people stared!) — and when she had understood at last that my interest in her was purely historical, then, very good-naturedly and satisfied perhaps with her constantly replenished glass, she summoned up old memories of Peter Kip.

"You've picked the right man for your thesis! A gentleman and a scholar if ever there was one. He was my last great love."

"You mean that you and he were lovers?" This may sound naive, but I still could not take it in. She was so awful!

"Of course we were. What else could we have been? He wanted me to give up modeling, except, of course, for him. He wanted to set me up in my own apartment with a trust fund for life. I think he would have married me if he'd been free. He had a kind of obsession about making me respectable. Oh, there was never a man so generous. He would have made me independent of everyone, even of himself!"

"But Florence," I gasped, "where are his paintings of you? Do you realize they could be the making of my thesis?"

"He destroyed them all!" she cried, flinging up her arms.

"Destroyed them? Why? Because they were so bad?"

"Bad? They were glorious! Oh, you should have seen me in those days! I was a dish for the gods, if I say so myself. Don't take my word for it. Go to the park and see . . . '

"Arethusa. I know. She's a beauty."

Florence grunted after eyeing me to be sure I wasn't kidding. "He destroyed them because I left him for a brute of a painter who didn't have a *sou* and beat me when he was drunk. But, oh God, could he make love! So I gave up a fortune, and for what? To be robbed and abandoned by a viper. It served me right. I sacrificed everything for my body, and my body's all I have left. Well, you've seen it, my friend!" At this she raised her hand toward the bartender for another refill.

Walking home that night, I saw the Kip interiors from a different point of view. Now all those wonderful creams and golds, those blended greens and grays, the silken softness of the cushions, the stillness of noon in the hot sunlight of the gardens outside the shaded libraries, the Cupids and Venuses in the Fragonard tapestries, the cool, inviting forests in the *fête-champêtre* watercolors on the walls, seemed to evoke the delights of a lost love, of a happiness so exquisite that it could only be mourned ever after in the kind of empty but enchanted chambers in which it had been enjoyed. Peter Kip had created a gallery to commemorate the greatest experience of his life, his only passion!

But Donald Cole did not allow me to indulge in these fantasies for long. He chuckled when I told him of the revelation in the bar.

"Well, I have no doubt the old girl bedded him, no matter how much he may have preferred the boys. But I'd take all that business about its being a great passion *cum grano salis*. Old Florence is subject to delusions of grandeur. I wouldn't be surprised if she told me that she'd passed up a chance to become Mrs. Picasso!" He shook his head almost ruefully now. "Still, I like that business about the trust fund. Florence could never have dreamed *that* up, so it's got to be true. Kip was certainly a very kind man. Who else would have thought of setting up an old tart for life?"

"Oh, no doubt he was compensating for something else," I retorted, unwilling now to share my Peter Kip with the likes of him.

Shortly after Florence's revelation, what I had dreaded all along took place. The Whitney Museum mounted a show of American realist painters of the nineteen thirties and forties and included a dozen Kips. This resulted in a spate of newspaper comments about him, mostly condescending, but with the marked exception of one discerning piece in *ArtNews* that spoke of the "curious quality of muffled emotion" that seemed to permeate the light from the windows, the gleam of the porcelains and the tint of bronze. At the end the writer waxed almost as lyrical as I had been:

It is not so much as if a person had just been in one of these rooms, as if a ghost had. There seems to have been — or perhaps still to be — a presence there. It might be that of someone who deeply senses the beauty of each unit and of their combination, a person who feels that these things may have a life of their own and who hankers to be a part of it. Or perhaps it is simply the presence of the painter himself.

The third morning that I attended the show I found myself alone in the Kip room except for an old gentleman in black with a malacca cane, a spotless gray felt hat in hand, a brown-spotted eaglelike countenance and thick, curly white hair. I felt immediately sure that he must have known Kip, and when we had both been in the chamber for half an hour, I summoned up the courage to ask him if he had.

"Oh, very well," he replied vigorously, not in the least surprised to be so accosted. "We were close friends for many years. Are you interested in his work? I suppose you must be, or you wouldn't have been here so long."

I explained to him what I was doing and asked him if he could shed any light on what I deemed the central mystery of the subject matter.

"There being no people, you mean? I think I might. Why don't I take you to lunch at my club? Are you free? It's only a few blocks away."

I felt a little odd about accepting, particularly as I wasn't wearing a tie, but Mr. Gurney, as my new friend was called, asked the man at the door of the Union Club to fetch one for me, and soon we were seated in the long dining room overlooking Park Avenue, consuming Chablis and omelet under the sober row of painted likenesses of the institution's past presidents. I had no difficulty in getting my host to talk. His more decorous memories flowed out as freely as Florence's. But in the end they turned unexpectedly sinister.

"We went to China together in 1937 and we happened to be in Shanghai on the very day it fell to the Japs. Fortunately, I had some important connections in Tokyo, and I was able to arrange for our transportation from the ill-fated city in an officer's car with an armed escort. What was rather less fortunate was that our driver, mistaking his route, took us through a square where we witnessed something we were not supposed to have seen. A group of wretched Chinese civilians, including a number of women, had been roped together in the middle of the square and presumably sprayed with gasoline, for just as we turned into the area the poor bundle of human faggots ignited. There was a hideous clamor of shouting and screaming; our car stalled, and the first thing I knew Kip was out of the vehicle, rushing toward the flames. He was actually trying to untie the rope, at imminent risk of burning himself to death, when he was seized by soldiers and returned to our car. He was unharmed, thank God, at least outwardly. I shall never forget the horror in his wild eyes and ashen face as our Japanese host, a colonel, tried to explain that the victims were terrorists, of whom an example had to be made. The curious thing was that Kip refused ever afterwards to discuss the incident, even with me. It had gone too deep, I suppose."

The old boy was silent at last, and for several seconds I stared at him.

"And you, sir? Did it go equally deep with you?"

Mr. Gurney raised his eyes to the ceiling. "Ah, my dear fellow, I'd been around the Orient. I knew what our little brown brothers were capable of. I'd seen even worse than that, believe me. Why, in Siam once . . ."

"Please, sir! I can't bear to hear any more!"

"Oh, very well. You young fellows are a squeamish lot. But just wait. You'll learn these things!"

"But tell me one more thing. Was *that* the reason he stopped putting human beings in his pictures? Because they were too vile?"

"Well, the dates fit, don't they?"

After lunch, when my wuthering old host went to snooze in the library, I returned to the Whitney. I knew just the painting that I wished to reexamine. It depicted a parlor in a great English country house, with elaborate white carved pilasters along the walls, an Aubusson carpet and a royal set of Louis XV armchairs and divans covered with needlepoint of glorious red with medallions of white cupids and flowers.

The red, although presumably the same in all the actual material, varied in the painting from a rich pink, like the *rose de Pompadour* of the porcelains, to a deep, dark ruby that was almost imperial purple, to, finally, a jumping, fiery scarlet in the cushions on the central divan. The effect on the placid chamber was like a fire in a grate. The middle of the picture seemed to throb until to my hallucinated eye it recalled that Japanese auto-da-fé. Was I at last on the threshold of an understanding of Peter Kip?

Had he turned in nausea from a world where man did such things to man to the blessed opiate of a world of perfect harmony? Had the half-open doors of his interiors just witnessed the exit of the monsters he could no longer bear to portray? Had he harnessed and tamed the fury of hell and contained it in the red of a sofa cushion? Ah, if a man could do *that*! Was it insanity to think it might mean that those poor souls had not died utterly in vain?

But it was with a deep groan that I recognized at last that my theory was too subjective for a thesis at New York University. It would never do for Donald Cole. I had better put away my notes and dust off last year's on the preabstract period of Kandinsky.

The Tender Offer

$\mathcal{V}$ALERIAN SHAW, a member of the flourishing midtown Manhattan corporate law firm of Treanor, Saunders, Arkdale, Rosen & Shaw, had long assumed that, by the time he should have reached the age of sixty-four, he would have achieved a modicum of emotional and financial security. Although, like most of his heavily taxed generation, he had scanty savings, he had figured that his ultimate pension should be adequate to keep him comfortably as a widower in his small apartment on Riverside Drive where, surrounded by his books and collection of New York iconography, he would be able peaceably to pursue to the grave his hobby of metropolitan history.

But in his sixty-fourth year, with only three to go before his mandatory retirement, a strange thing happened. He began to lose his professional nerve. Valerian found himself now uncomfortably conscious of a widening discrepancy between the pace of his working efforts and that of his partners and associates. The image that seemed to stick in his mind was of them all engaged in a forced march across the slushy bog of the endless legal technicalities of the seventies, a quagmire of statutes and regulations and judicial opinions, and of himself sticking in the slime, falling behind the resolutely progressing backs of the others. He began at last to be afraid that he would not be able to pull his weight in the firm until the retirement age.

And then, as if to justify this gloomy foreboding, the basket in which for thirty years he had toted most of his legal eggs burst its bottom and dropped its cargo on the street. Standard Bank & Trust Company, the small but reliable depository of the fortunes of some of New York's oldest families for which he had so long labored, first as an associate and then as a partner, on whose board of directors he had conscientiously served, and all of whose principal officers he had come to regard as his particular friends, was merged, taken over, consumed, raped, by First National Merchants' Loan. The new amalgamate ("Thank you very much, old Val!") would be quite adequately represented in the future by Lockridge, Kelly, First National's old-time, hard-nosed legal experts, who had designed the plan that had resulted in Standard's sudden siege and quick, fluttering surrender.

Valerian at first tried desperately to persuade himself that the blow was not a fatal one to his position in the firm. Might another bank not seek a general retainer? Might his friends at Standard not yet gain control of the amalgamate? And surely he had other clients. Was the vault not full of wills? The partners were very kind. But it was a matter not of months but of weeks, and very few of them, before the computer began remorselessly to show the steady increase of unbilled time and the widening discrepancy between the overhead of Valerian's little department and the revenues that it engendered. He could not fool himself that he would long escape that "soul-searching" interview with the senior partner.

Cecil Treanor and Valerian had been classmates at Andover, Yale and Harvard Law, but Cecil was not a man to be too much counted on, even by so old an acquaintance. He had a convenient way of packing noble ends with rather less noble means in the same box without any seeming awareness of the least impropriety or even inconsistency. At Yale, for example, he had written a series of controversial columns for the *News* attacking the powerful senior societies, only to end by accepting the bid of Skull and Bones. At law school he had composed a brilliant note for the *Review* on legal restraints to anti-Semitism, and had then joined a club in Boston that excluded Jews. Years later, as president of the New York State Bar Association, he had thunderously preached the gospel of *pro bono publico* while keeping his own clerks so busy they hadn't a minute left for the needy. And always these compromises, if such they were, seemed to be effected without any interrupting cough in that emphatic tone, without the interposition of a single cloud over that beaming countenance. Sometimes of late Valerian had begun to feel that that beam was more like a hard electric light.

That Cecil should come to Valerian's office for the soul-searching talk was in itself indicative of its importance, but his tone was milder than Valerian had expected.

"We've never been just a 'money firm,' and we're never, at least while I'm around, going to be one. We measure a partner's contribution by many factors other than the fees he brings in. In your case, Val, there are qualities of experience and wisdom and compassion and integrity — yes, sir, good old-fashioned integrity — that are indispensable to a firm like ours. Some of our younger partners don't know the value of those things, but they'll learn."

"It's good of you to say that, Cecil."

"Nonsense! You and I go back together to the flood. One doesn't forget that. But, as Hamlet said to Horatio, 'something too much of this.' What I came in to suggest, now that you have a little more time on your hands, is that maybe you could help me out a bit."

"In what?" Val was instantly alert.

"Well, how about giving me a hand on a new piece of business?" Cecil paused here to assume a graver look. "My client

Zolex is casting a hungry eye in the direction of Pilgrim Publishers."

"Pilgrim! But that's one of the finest houses in the book business! What does Zolex know about literature?"

"Oh, Zolex knows a bit about everything. Don't forget they acquired the Heller chain last year. Department stores sell books, don't they?"

"I suppose they do." Val saw the sudden gleam in his partner's eye and knew that he must be careful. "Simeon Andrews in Pilgrim is an old friend of mine."

"I'm aware of that." Cecil was watching him carefully now. "I thought that might come in handy. You've always taken an interest in publishing, have you not?"

"Oh, nothing special." Val began to feel very nervous. "Not enough to be any real help to you. Frankly, Cecil, I don't see myself working on a corporate takeover. Even the vocabulary gets me down. Terms like 'bear hug' and 'blitzkrieg' and 'shark repellent'!"

But there was no answering smile from Cecil. "*I* use those terms, Val. They are merely technical. Are you suggesting there is anything illegal about the acquisition by Zolex of a controlling share of Pilgrim's common stock?"

"Oh, no, of course not."

"Are you suggesting, then, that I am violating any of the canons of ethics by advising Zolex how most expeditiously to acquire that stock within the law?"

"No, no, you're perfectly ethical. I guess it's the huggermugger of the whole thing that sticks in my craw. The way we go about it. First checking the files to see if we have ever had any legal connection with the target company. And then the stealthy lining up of stockholders and the secret approaches. And finally — *bang* — the unleashing of the tender offer, like a Pearl Harbor attack!"

"Of course, if it's all so distasteful to you, you needn't have anything to do with it. I can see I'm wasting your time."

"No, please, Cecil, of course I'll do it! I'm just shooting my big mouth off. You know how I am."

Cecil nodded briskly to accept his partner's collapse. It had been wholly anticipated. He then proceeded to a more delicate matter: a proposed fifty percent reduction in Valerian's share of the firm's profits. This was accompanied by what was known jocularly among the partners as the "old fart" formula: "We old farts have to keep moving over to make room for the younger men!"

But Val knew perfectly well that only one old fart would be taking the cut.

*   *   *

Nothing had added more to Valerian's malaise in the firm than Cecil's development of a large department, highly trained and specialized, to be dedicated to the art of corporate acquisitions. When the practice of company raiding on a large scale had begun, Cecil had denounced it as dirty business, and had loftily told his partners at a firm lunch that they should act only as defenders in such cases. The "snide art," he stoutly maintained, of preparing and launching a surprise attack against some unsuspecting company, whose officers, about to be stripped of their livelihood, might like as not be numbered among one's closest friends, ill fitted gentlemen supposedly devoted to the pursuit of justice and the reverence of law. But when Cecil's own corporate clients had begun to look to other firms for just this service, he had performed more than a volte-face. He had made his firm the first in the field! Like Philippe-Égalité in the French Revolution, he wore the lilies of France on his liberty cap with perfect aplomb. History to Cecil, Valerian sometimes mused, must have seemed like a fancy-dress ball. Was there any reason that Justice

Holmes and Al Capone should not have had a friendly drink together?

Valerian was somewhat relieved to discover that his role in the preparation of Zolex's project was confined to a study of all the material on Pilgrim Publishers that the firm had been able, with the necessary discretion, to lay its hands on. He did not quite see what value this would have in a proxy fight, but Cecil assured him that he needed someone at hand with the overall picture in mind. He suspected that the senior partner might be making up work for him, but even if this were so, why should he complain? He only hoped that he would not have to be present at any meeting, once the matter became public, with his old friend Simeon Andrews.

Ordinarily he lunched with the editor of Pilgrim every couple of weeks, but now he discontinued the practice, and at his club in the Pan Am Building he frequented the buffet, knowing that his friend was apt to lunch in the main dining room. But one day at noon, crossing the lobby, he felt a firm pull on his sleeve and turned to confront the countenance that he had been avoiding.

"Where have you been hiding, Val?" Simeon demanded. "I've been looking out for you all week."

"I've been having a sandwich sent in to my office. I'm keeping pretty busy these days, Sim."

"Too busy for a little business talk? Too busy for a proposition I want to put to you? How about the regular dining room? I hate just to eat and run."

Valerian submissively followed his friend to the latter's regularly reserved table in a corner of the green-walled room hung with Audubon prints. Simeon's table was directly under a print that depicted two red-tailed hawks fighting in the air over a bleeding rabbit clutched by one. Valerian, unpleasantly reminded of the impending fate of Pilgrim, shuddered. Was it possible that Simeon had got wind of the raid?

But Simeon seemed wholly absorbed in gravely applying a piece of lemon peel to the rim of his pre-iced martini glass. Bald, wide-eyed, he was as still, except for his moving fingers, as some great bird of prey on a bare limb. Valerian had always associated this stillness with his friend's reputation for being able to pick the best as well as the most popular books without even reading them. His secret, Simeon used to boast, was that if his eyes were sometimes closed, his mind was always open. Nothing was too refined, too esoteric, too vulgar, or too pornographic for his consideration.

"Do you remember, Val, that you once mentioned to me that it would be a great idea if some house were to publish the unexpurgated diaries of Philip Hone and George Templeton Strong in a joint edition?"

"Why, yes," Valerian replied, astonished at his friend's memory. "Allan Nevins published only half of each of them. And Strong really begins where Hone leaves off. Put together, they'd make a week-by-week, almost a day-by-day account of life in New York from eighteen twenty-five to eighteen seventy-five."

"Precisely. Well, that idea of yours stuck in my mind. That's how a good publisher operates. Those fifty years represent the transition of New York from a minor seaport to a great metropolis. By eighteen seventy-six the job was pretty well done. Fifth Avenue boasted as many châteaux as the Loire Valley, and all the great cultural institutions had been founded or at least planned."

"And do you know something else, Sim? I've read the manuscripts of those diaries in the New-York Historical Society. The unpublished parts are just as good as the published. Nevins simply had to cut because his editors wouldn't give him the space he needed. But imagine, if he'd had an editor with your vision!"

Simeon sipped his drink complacently. "Well, I've been looking into it. It seems to me perfectly feasible. I don't say it would be a great money-maker, but any publishing house that's worth its salt should be willing to stick its neck out from time to time. We owe it to the public. We owe it to history!"

"Oh, Sim, that's wonderful!"

"*If* we decide to go ahead with it, would you consider serving on some kind of advisory board? On questions of how much explanatory text we need and how many footnotes? We wouldn't be able to pay you much, but then, it shouldn't take too much of your time."

"Pay me! I'd pay *you* for the privilege! My God, man, this project has been my dream of dreams!"

Simeon smiled, pleased at such a display of enthusiasm, although probably considering it a bit on the naive side. But Valerian didn't care. He ordered a second martini, although he knew it would make him tiddly in the middle of the day. He began to calculate how many volumes would be needed — not too many, not more than ten. His mind was already a gallery of possible illustrations. His second cocktail came, and he swallowed it in a couple of minutes. He started to run off to his friend the names of possible editors . . .

And then, when Simeon had suddenly sprung up from the table to buttonhole a former mayor whose memoirs he had his eye on, a terrible thought came to Valerian. The radiant dome of his new fantasy was shattered.

Zolex!

Was it conceivable that a massive corporate conglomerate, controlled by men concerned with profit and profit alone, would countenance such a project? Of course not! The mere suggestion might cost its proponent his job.

Valerian deliberately reached over now to pick up Simeon's half-finished cocktail, and finished it for him. His heart was beating rapidly, and the big crowded room blurred before his eyes. Through his mind throbbed the slow, marching melody of the old hymn: "Once to-o ev-er-y man a-a-and na-a-tion, comes the-e-e mo-o-ment to-o decide." Simeon came back to the table.

"Sorry, old boy, but I had to have a word with Tom. He's given me an option on his autobio. Of course, he can't write a word of English. Seen any good ghosts lately?"

"Simeon!" Valerian exclaimed sharply and then abruptly paused. His friend eyed him curiously.

"What is it, Val?"

Valerian seemed to be looking at the editor from the other side of a deep crevice. Could he jump it? Would he stumble? He lowered his eyes to the tablecloth as with an audible gasp he took the mental leap. But he fell! He fell and fell!

"Val, are you feeling all right?"

Valerian looked up, dazed, from the bottom of his pit. "I'm all right, Sim," he said in a flat voice. "I want to tell you something about a client of ours."

Simeon's big watery eyes stared as he listened to Valerian's tale in absolute silence. But when the latter had finished, and the editor responded, his tone was curiously emotionless. He shook his head.

"Well, I'll be damned. It seems we live in a new age of piracy. Thanks for the tip, old boy."

"Of course, you realize I've put my professional life in your hands."

Simeon gave him a shrewd look. "Of course I do," he said softly. "But never fear. I shall be discreet. And now, I think, everything points to a very good lunch."

Valerian reflected that it was indicative of the strength of the man that he could even think of lunch at such a moment! He tried to quell the rising surge of panic in his stomach by telling himself that he had only done his duty as a friend. And as a citizen. And as a student of New York history.

* * *

Valerian soon heard at the office that somebody besides Zolex scouts was picking up Pilgrim stock, but this was not an unusual development. No matter how secret a raider's precautions, there were always nostrils keen enough to pick up the scent of impending war. What disturbed him was that the lawyers working on the matter did not seem more disturbed. The general expectation that Pilgrim would go down with only a few bubbles continued unabated.

On the Sunday afternoon before the filing of the tender offer Valerian took a long walk with his frayed and shaggy poodle in Central Park. As he circled the reservoir and let his eyes rest on the southern skyline, his mood was one of static resignation. It seemed to him now that his little gesture was merely symbolic of his own uselessness and futility in the modern world. There was no law but that of the market, no right but that of the strong. The irresistible and unresisted materialism of the day was a flooding river that had penetrated every fissure and cranny of his world, inundating poor and rich, unions and management, the most popular entertainment and the greatest art. He visualized, tossing on its raging surface, the torn pages of the diaries of Philip Hone and George Templeton Strong.

On Monday he did not go to the office until the afternoon. He had no function in the filing of the tender offer or in the subsequent call on the target. Was it his imagination that the receptionist's greeting was saucy?

"Mr. Treanor wants to see you immediately, Mr. Shaw. He said for you to go right in the moment you arrived."

Valerian, his overcoat on his arm, his heart pounding, entered the office of the senior partner. Cecil jumped up at once, without greeting him, and strode to the window where he stood with his back to his visitor.

"How did things go at Pilgrim, Cecil?"

"Very well, no thanks to you," the bitter voice came back to Valerian. "In fact, I've never seen a smoother takeover. They capitulated at once. It was positively friendly! Your friend,

Simeon Andrews, played his cards with the greatest astuteness. He sold his own stock for ten million plus an agreement that he would be chairman of the board of Zolex-Pilgrim for three years! It seems to be a question of who took over whom!"

Valerian felt his panic ebb away as he stood silently contemplating the wide, tweeded back of his former friend and about-to-be former partner. He took in the surprising fact that he was not surprised. There was something almost comforting in the flatness, the totality of his desolation.

"Andrews had another condition," the voice continued. "If we are to continue as counsel to Zolex-Pilgrim, the price will be your resignation from this firm. He informed me all about your indiscretion. He had already flared the Zolex project, so you told him nothing he didn't know, but he says he cannot afford to be represented by a firm with such a leak. Of course, I had to agree with him. I told him that you would cease to be a member of the firm as of today. I assured him that, if you refused to resign, we would dissolve the firm and re-form without you."

"That won't be necessary, Cecil. I resign. As of this moment."

Cecil whirled around. "How could you do it, Val?" There was actually some feeling in his voice now. "How could you do it to me? After all I've done for you? Looking after you and inventing things for you to do? And saving your stupid neck from our ravenous younger partners?"

"There's no point talking about it."

"Of course, I'll have to tell the firm about it. I'm afraid there can be no idea now of a regular pension. But if you will let me negotiate the matter for you, I'll see that you get something. We don't want you to starve, after all. I'll put it to the partners as a kind of aberration on your part. Perhaps even that you've had a small stroke."

"Any way you want it, Cecil. I leave that entirely to you."

"But, Val, how *could* you?" Cecil's voice now rose to a wail.

"How could you betray a client? How could you violate the most sacred of the canons of ethics? What are the younger men to think of us? When I tell them at firm meetings what the ideals of Treanor, Saunders mean to me, to clients, to the bar, to the public? Won't they simply laugh at me?"

"I guess they may, Cecil," Valerian replied wearily as he turned now to the door. "I guess they really may. Why don't you just tell them you've gotten rid of a rotten egg?"

Marley's Chain

THE CHRISTMAS OF 1936 would have been the first Christmas that Leslie Fairburn had spent at home in fifteen years. Diplomatic posts had been responsible for most of these absences from his beloved Castle in Charlottesville, but there had also been the factor of his old bachelor's distaste for the season of stockings and screaming infants, which had helped to render him immune, for that brief season at least, from the lure of the blue hills and red earth of his native Virginia. But now that he had retired from the diplomatic service and come home to stay, it would have appeared, when the end of December came around, not only unfriendly to his neighbors to go away, but, considering all of their many kindnesses and hospitalities in welcoming him back, downright boorish. Particularly when Miss Matilda Bulloch had asked him to read aloud Dickens's *Christmas Carol* at her annual gathering for all ages on the twenty-fourth. It was a signal honor.

Mattie Bulloch had reached the age that he had reached, fifty-four, but he liked to think that time had been kinder to him. It was not that she was not what was called "a fine figure of a woman"; she was, almost to a fault. But she was big and hefty and broad-shouldered, with frizzy gray hair and a square head with fine large features that made Leslie think of some heroic bust, some staring, broad-browed Beethoven or Daniel Webster, in a public park. Nobody in the county was more widely respected than "Miss Mattie"; it was as if the spirit of the Confederate battle leaders had found its appropriate abode in the heart of this indomitable old maid. Though poor — the little white house with the white columns that she inhabited with one ancient black woman was almost crumbling — Miss Bulloch was the chairman of every local charitable drive and the acknowledged arbiter of social forms and precedences. That she was to some extent a law to herself she would admit proudly to the visitor who presumed to stare, finding her shelling peas on her front porch, and retort: "Well, if a Carter's Hill Bulloch can't shell peas on her own front porch, who can?"

It was an established legend that Leslie Fairburn had been the love of her life, and that he had reciprocated her passion only with friendship, albeit a deep and enduring one. They were second cousins, twice or three times over in the old Virginia way, and had been childhood playmates, but there had been always the difference of Leslie's romantic good looks and of his family's wealth, Richmond-acquired, which had made him the catch of the county, far beyond the reach of a poor, plain girl, for all her goodness and character. And Leslie, as romantic in soul as in his soft gray-blue eyes, had fallen in love with a Tidewater beauty who had died of tuberculosis during the period of their engagement, leaving him to sworn sorrow and a diplomatic career where he could dream in foreign cities of the radiant lost bride in diamonds who seemed to have been born to be an ambassadress.

Leslie's retirement in his early fifties had been ostensibly for the purpose of devoting himself to the writing of a book on foreign affairs, but it had in fact been the result of a severe nervous depression. This had started with his small but persistent suspicion that the balance sheet of his life was showing an unduly fat sum of personal pleasures and privileges in contrast to the exiguous one of what he had contributed to the world. Why, he found himself increasingly asking, should he have been endowed with such fine looks, such radiant health, so great a fortune and so interesting a life in European capitals, and, to cap it all, the rare talent of enjoying all these things, while his fellow mortals struggled with poverty, disease and neurasthenia? Why had he been singled out for so many blessings? What had he ever given back?

The few friends in whom he confided these doubts tried to persuade him that he was undergoing some kind of male change of life, and that it would soon enough pass. But it didn't, and he began at last to wonder if he could face his daily task with the proper zeal and the necessary detachment. A first leave of absence led to a second and then to his precipitate retirement. He hoped to find in his Castle relief from his tormenting obsession.

Virginia, however, seemed only to intensify his ailment. What, he now put to his inner mentor, had he done to justify the perfection of the great cool rooms, the gleaming eighteenth-century furniture, the rich, dark paneling that provided so fine a setting for his collection of French paintings? Why for him had fate provided the modern model farm, the picturesque herd of black Angus, the amiable staff of efficient servants? And he did not even suffer from the habitual boredom of the rich! He was not even lonely! But for this terrible new conscience, he would have been perfectly happy with his books and pictures, his horses and dogs.

Something of this mood he attempted at last to convey to Mattie Bulloch, after his reading of *A Christmas Carol,* when the neighbors and nephews and cousins had departed, and she had lingered by the fire in her parlor for a nightcap and a comfortable chat. For, yes, that was yet another of his blessings, if blessings they really were. It *would* be a comfortable chat. So fully had Mattie accepted the impossibility of any romance between them that he was never uneasy with her. He owned her, as he owned his herd of Angus.

"I was not entirely happy reading tonight," he observed.

"Did you think you weren't doing it well?" Mattie asked in surprise. "I never heard you better. I could almost hear the chain of Marley's ghost clanking up the stairway. It gave me goose pimples!"

"So did it me. That's the point. I identified with Ebenezer Scrooge. I *was* Ebenezer Scrooge." He paused, now eyeing her intently. "Has it ever occurred to you, Mattie, that I *am* Ebenezer Scrooge?"

"Well, you're hardly a miser." Her tone rejected his more serious one. "You might be better off if you were, a little. At the rate you're spending, my dear!"

"But all on myself, don't you see? Haven't I forgotten, like Jacob Marley, that mankind is my business?"

"I suppose you were spending money on yourself when you put my nephew Tommy through V.M.I.? And when you sent my niece Effie around the world after her marriage broke up?"

"But what did those things cost me? Did I have to give up a single painting? Even a single drawing?"

"There are still plenty of rich people who don't pick up other people's bills."

"Maybe so. But there are plenty of Scrooges, too. Mattie, what lasting contribution have I made to the world?"

Mattie began to be fretted. "As much as any of the rest of us. More. What about the art collection that you're leaving to the university? What about your little book on Jefferson's last years in Monticello? Isn't it considered a minor classic? Not even to mention all the things you've done for your country abroad!"

"I can't seem to make you see it," he protested, struck by the solid wall of apparent accomplishment in which he seemed to have encased himself. "All those things are simply extensions of my ego."

"Isn't that true of everyone?"

"Not of you, dear. You live for others."

There was nothing coy in Mattie's frank snort. "I take life as it comes, and I advise you to do the same. Has it never occurred to you, Leslie Fairburn, that you may be one of those whose mission it is to *accept* blessings? 'Only God's free gifts abuse not,' the old hymn reads."

"But I *have* abused them!"

"Oh, go home!" Mattie exclaimed roughly as she now rose. "I'm off to bed. Merry Christmas!"

Leslie went home and had a drink; he even had two, before he went to bed, but then he slept only fitfully and had bad dreams. It seemed to him, all night, that he heard the clank of Marley's chain on the stairway, and when it was dragged at last into his chamber by a ghost looking like himself, he saw that it was hauling a long train of heavy, beautiful, dead things: pictures in gilded frames, porcelains and ivory figures, cumbersome old folios, beakers and platters of enamel, of silver, of gold, and the undecayed carcasses of splendid beasts. And it was too late, somehow too late, for redemption. He knew that he would have to drag his collection through eternity!

Christmas dawn found him sitting shivering by an open window. He had a strange, dull hope that some answer might come to him with the sun. And, indeed, with the first red slants of light over the black trees and the gray lawn he felt his whole body surging with the sudden fever of a great idea. What if he were to offer his hand, his fortune, his farm, his art collection and all that was left of his life and heart to poor dear Mattie Bulloch?

* * *

There was only one person to whom he could speak of his project before speaking to Mattie herself, and that was Hilda Warren. She had moved from New York with her husband, Slater Warren, a retired banker some years older than herself, to spend their well-earned leisure in a beautiful old house, Box Grove, that they had purchased and tastefully done over. But no sooner had they settled in it than Warren had suddenly died, and Leslie, who had come home on leave shortly thereafter, had found many occasions of being useful to the brave and charming widow. A close friendship had grown up between them, carried on by correspondence when he returned to foreign posts. It had been his pleasant theory that they had achieved a rare understanding and communication, independent of family ties or romantic complications. It was certainly his duty, that very Christmas morn, to inform her of any step that might abrogate their arrangement.

Box Grove, like so many early nineteenth-century houses in Albemarle County, was reputed to have benefited from Mr. Jefferson's architectural genius, and indeed its main floor and concealed second floor, its curious amalgamation of red-brick wings and its small central cupola, were reminiscent of Monticello. Inside it was small, compact and charming. Hilda had filled the living room with fine federal furniture, and when she presided, as now, over a coffee urn of George II silver, the effect was all that even as sophisticated an observer as Leslie could wish.

She was a small, bright, darting woman of fifty, as restless as a spring warbler and as colorful in her attire. Though her taste was perfect, there seemed no end of her efforts to improve, with a touch or a twist, her rooms, her clothes, her life. She wore no aspect of mourning for the husband to whom she had supposedly been devoted except in the shining blackness of her eyes and hair. She had never been beautiful, but she knew so much about beauty that she seemed to be. Oddly, for such a tense and mobile woman, she was a sympathetic listener. She could handle a silver tongs or blow out a match in such a way as to enhance one's impression of her attention.

That morning, over the coffee cups, she listened to Leslie with an intentness that seemed to betray an indecision as to what her reaction should be. But when Leslie had finished and was waiting for her response, she composed herself, like a monologuist about to embark on a characterization. She clasped her hands, holding them up before her face, as at the wonder of his news.

"Matilda Bulloch! Let it never be said of you, Leslie, that you are not a master of the unexpected."

"Oh, of course, I know people will laugh. But people like to laugh. Where's the harm in that?"

"To them? Very little. I was thinking of Mattie."

"Oh, they won't laugh at *her*. They'll laugh at me. But I shan't care. I must stop thinking of myself, that's just the point. The danger of my scheme is that it may tend even to accentuate my egotism."

"You mean by making you think too much about your own selfishness? Because of the task you have had to set yourself to redeem it?"

"Yes! It's not, of course, that I'm not guilty of a long lifetime of selfishness. Oh, I am! But I mustn't revel in it, don't you see? I mustn't just dwell on my own collection of crimes."

"Yes, I think I begin to see it," she mused. "It would make you a kind of connoisseur of your own wickednesses. One might see you taking friends down the long gallery and saying, 'Now here's a very fine little sin that I picked up in Hong Kong for a song.'"

He smiled. "I was right to talk to you. You *do* see it."

"Oh, yes, I see that you must quash that ego! You must learn to concentrate on others!" She paused. "But is Mattie Bulloch really others?"

"Well, a lot of people come with her, nephews and nieces and the like. She has a great collection of lame ducks that I can help."

Hilda seemed to consider this. "And I suppose it's a foregone conclusion that she will accept you?"

"Well, if she turns me down, I'll still, you see, have made my offer."

"And got off scot free! But never fear. She won't. She will, of course, be overjoyed."

"Well, think of all I can do for her," he murmured, deprecating her tone.

"And all she can do for *you*. Don't you count on the joy that *her* joy will bring you?"

"Oh, I see where you're coming out!" he exclaimed. "That under the great act of unselfishness lurks the biggest selfishness of all! That having lived my life for myself as long as I could, I am now making provision for my old age in the form of a strong, loving handmaiden!"

"I merely toy with the idea."

"Then let me assure you that I have plumbed my own dark depths more deeply than you think. Nor have I observed your sex all these years without making some notes. I am quite aware, for example, of the strength of women's resentments. It is manifest in the speed with which even the plainest one, if a husband comes her way, learns to take him for granted. Why not? In the war between the sexes what proud female cares to be an Uncle Tom? I quite see that Mattie may turn out to be a bit of a tyrant."

"Even perhaps a bit of a shrew?"

"No. The tyrant would be enough," he answered with a hint of reproach.

"And don't forget her causes! The old Confederate causes! Oh, the Castle will reek with meetings. But that, of course, will be the daily proof of your redemption. Of your saved soul. Yes, the tyrant will be even better than the handmaiden. Wait till she hangs her battle paintings in your gallery!" At last he winced, and he saw that she saw it. "But we mustn't think that it will all be difficult," she continued. "Won't there be the joy that Scrooge felt in his heart when he woke up and found that it was still Christmas Day?"

"Ah, yes, I do permit myself that thought," he confessed

eagerly. "That sudden filling of the heart to bursting with the idea that it's not too late!"

"And what was the first thing Scrooge did? Let me see. Oh, yes, the very first thing he did was to open the window and call to the boy in the street..."

"To buy the biggest goose at the grocer's for the Cratchetts!"

"Just so! And you will do that, my dear." She leaned back in her chair and now gave utterance to a high, shrill laugh. "But no matter how big a goose you buy, there'll be a bigger one left in the store!"

He stared. "And that is me?"

"No, *me!* For not foreseeing that you would fall into a pit like this!"

* * *

Leslie was much disturbed by Hilda's reaction. It was not so much her calling him a goose that he minded; that had been in the cards. He had expected it; he had even rather looked forward to being called a goose by a woman so charming. But what he could not get over was her calling herself one. The only implication that he could possibly draw from this was that Hilda considered herself a goose for not having anticipated and headed off his idea of marrying Mattie, and how could she have done that without in some way placing herself in Mattie's position, at least as the object of any belated Fairburn matrimonial intent? But was this consistent with her reputation of being a priestess dedicated to the ashes of the deceased? Or was he a simple fool? Weren't women *always* inconsistent?

The sudden vision of a life with Hilda was like a dazzling revelation. Was it conceivable that anything so wonderful could happen to a man of his age, with his past? That after decades of living, so to speak, off the fat of the land, he should simply have reserved for his autumnal years the finest prize of the harvest? That like some battered old sea lion, instead of retiring to a lonely rock, bitten and chased off by the younger bulls, he should lead proudly past their frustrated muzzles the finest cow of the herd? But what chain would be long enough for the ghost of such a man to drag behind him into a revenging eternity?

At Christmas dinner at Mattie Bulloch's he could think of nothing else. The walls of her dining room were decorated by the rather primitive mural of a painter nephew, depicting the great houses of the neighborhood, her visits to which, she used to remark with a toss of her head, had been interdicted by their sale to rich Yankees. Of course she exaggerated furiously, for she always had gone, and still went, everywhere, and now he drew her attention to the fact that she had dined only the week before with Hilda Warren.

"Isn't it better," he continued argumentatively, "that these fine old pieces should pass to persons who can afford to keep them up? Even you, Mattie, must admit that Hilda has made a charming thing of Box Grove."

"She's gussied it up, if that's what you mean. I liked it the way it was."

"But surely it was falling to pieces!"

"It was shabby, I suppose. But shabby things survive. Look at my poor shack! Now Box Grove is all cute and perfect, like Hilda herself."

"Oh, come now, Mattie, won't you even concede her a bit of charm?"

"Two bits, if you like. If it's charm that makes the world go round, she should keep it spinning!"

Leslie renounced the obviously idle pursuit of a compliment for Hilda and turned to the pursuit of information. Of that Mattie had always a copious supply. "You must have known her husband. What was he really like?"

Mattie shrugged her big shoulders. "A silent type. On the surly side. Purse-proud, I'd say. A typical New Yorker."

"But she was devoted to him, I gather."

"*Do* you gather it? How can one tell with a woman who, as you say, is so charming?"

"You mean her charm is just a mask?"

"Well, isn't Yankee charm usually?"

"Mattie, you're incorrigible. Do you really believe that Hilda Warren is incapable of sincerity?"

"Incapable? No. But why should she bother to be? Doesn't she get everything she wants the way she is?"

"How do you know what she wants?"

"Well, I'll grant her this. She only wants the best. She's not like so many Yankee women — taken in by trumpery trash."

* * *

Early the next morning Hilda telephoned Leslie to ask if he could stop at her house on his morning ride. She had need, she explained, of his advice in an important matter that had just come up. He ordered his horse to be saddled immediately, and in less than half an hour he was in her parlor. He found Hilda standing alone in the middle of the room, as if she had just been puzzling something out.

"Ah!" she exclaimed. "How good of you to come so promptly. I need you badly."

"I am always at the disposal of a beautiful damsel in distress."

But she brought him at once to her serious purpose with a little clap of her hands. "Tell me, have you popped the question yet?"

"Oh, no. I'm not so precipitate. At my age one steps gingerly in such alien fields."

"Then we must back each other up. You must help me to pop mine!"

He stared at her stupidly. "What on earth are you talking about?"

"Simply that you have set me a great example. I see now that it will be my redemption to marry Harry Hobson."

He could not make out, in the limpid depths of those smiling eyes, whether she was laughing at him. But there was nothing of amusement about the slow thin cut across his heart. "And who in the name of wonder is Harry Hobson?"

"An old and faithful friend who proposed to me at dancing school in New York when we were both fourteen. And again at the Yale prom, six years later. I turned him down, and he married the girl next door, on what my vanity has always insisted must have been the rebound. She died the same year as Slater."

He decided that he must not look too somber. "And why cannot the still-passionate Mr. Hobson be the popper of his own question?"

"Because, poor dear, he's too much of a gentleman. Oh, yes, I know more than one!"

"And gentlemen don't propose? Of course, I admit, I haven't. Yet."

She paused for just a moment, as if to adjust to a graver note. "Not when they've had strokes."

The sliding blade along his heart was like the cutting edge of an iceberg. It would run the full length, through all his watertight compartments.

"He's had a stroke?" he repeated blankly.

"Oh, but it hasn't affected his mind," she reassured him. "Just his speech. But I've got so I can make out almost everything he says."

"And where have you learned that skill?"

"On my visits to New York. I see him every couple of months. At his little house in Rye."

"Little? So, presumably, you plan to bring him down here?" He looked vaguely around, as if seeing the house for the first time. "It's a charming spot for an invalid."

"Oh, no, there can be no idea of that!" she exclaimed. "You don't know the terms of Slater's horrid will?"

It was the first time, he reflected, that she had intimated that there had been anything "horrid" about Slater. "No. How should I?"

"My poor husband was always madly jealous. I lose Box Grove and half my income if I remarry."

"And Mr. Hobson isn't . . . isn't well provided for?"

"Oh, there'd be enough for two — and the nurses. If we're careful. We won't, of course, need the night nurse."

Leslie decided that he did not want to think about that. "I had always thought of you as an inconsolable widow. One whose principal light had gone out with her husband. That the charm and loveliness were all there but not the heart." He paused in sudden embarrassment. "Forgive me. I don't know why I'm so personal."

"Forgive you? But I adore it!" Again she clapped her hands. "The image of Andromache is just what I tried to create. You'd have put a hundred miles between yourself and an attractive, consolable widow. Oh, I know you, Leslie!"

"You mean . . . you mean that you *were* consolable?"

"Well, I don't mean that I was looking for a husband, if that's what you're so crudely implying. But I saw no reason to scare away *all* the eligible males of the county. After all, a lady likes to be able to give a dinner party."

"And now you won't be giving any more." Once again he looked sadly about, as at his lost opportunities. "Perhaps Mr. Hobson will be too much of a gentleman to accept."

"Left to himself, no doubt he would be. But he has a married daughter, with three small children, who lives next door. She's very dutiful but also very overworked. Catch her letting the likes of me get away!"

He sighed. "You make it all seem very dreary."

"You mean *you* make it all seem dreary. What on earth is it, my dear old friend, but the golden chance to turn a useless life into a useful one?"

"Your life is not useless!" His sudden bitterness choked him, and he roamed speechlessly about the room. By the bay window was her small, elegant writing desk, on curved spindly legs, and stacked on it neatly were her morning letters, ready to be mailed.

"Have you written to him?" he asked suddenly.

"I told you I had not yet popped."

"But is that only because you haven't mailed the letter?" Suddenly, rudely, he snatched up the top envelope. It was addressed to Henry Hobson. He actually brandished it at her. "Is this it?"

She smiled, in great amusement. "Why don't you open it and see?"

"May I?"

"Go ahead."

"It's a trick! The whole business is a trick! To make a fool of me!"

"Then you'd be very silly to read my letter."

"If you'll let me read it, will you let me destroy it?"

"How violent you are, Leslie! Destroy my poor letter?"

He walked over to the little fire under the square marble mantel and paused before it. Then, leaning down, slowly and deliberately, he placed it on the blaze. They both were silent. He turned to her.

"I don't care if it's a trick or not. It's opened my eyes. If you marry anyone, it has to be me!"

She said nothing; she smiled, but he had the feeling that the windows had been thrown open, and he wondered, in the imagined thrust of bracing air, if it might not still be Christmas Day. Whether he had redeemed himself or simply added the last and heaviest golden ball to the chain of his damnation he did not know. But he did know that he no longer cared.

The Artistic Personality

*I*N 1923 WORTHINGTON WHITSON had been living in Florence for almost a quarter of a century, and his tall trim figure, fine white hair, wrinkled brown face and cold blue eyes made up an image almost as familiar to street vendors as the statues in the Loggia dei Lanzi. His daily walk from his small bachelor's apartment in a fourteenth-century palazzo on the Via Tornabuoni, across the Arno and as far as the Pitti, was something that could be counted on like the mail or newspaper. His visits to galleries and antiquaries, like his lunches, were apt to be solitary, but in the evenings he was a great diner-out and a favorite extra man among the widowed ladies, titled and untitled, of the expatriate community.

Whitson was considered all things that an elegant New York gentleman of the Mauve Decade should have been: poised, articulate, grave, gentle, with exquisite manners and a positive erudition on all questions of social precedence. And he had been, too, in his day, something more than what his younger critics sneeringly called a walking book of etiquette; he had been, for a decade at least, the "gray eminence" behind Mrs. Darius Slocum and the acknowledged *arbiter elegantiarum* of Fifth Avenue and Newport. A world war and new ways might have caused a new generation to sneer at such things, but in Florence there were still enough who remembered that vanished world to compose a society in which such an anachronism as Whitson could comfortably flourish.

If Whitson had a fault, it was a venial one. He tended to wax a touch boring on the subject of the degeneration of American manners, even in a community not famous for its enthusiasm for Yankee ways.

"Don't let old Worthington get going on the subject of New York society," a hostess would murmur to a newcomer. "He gets too angry to be funny. Of course, it's all sour grapes. A young writer called Alistair Temple persuaded Euphemia Slocum to give him the sack. But he fancies himself Napoleon on St. Helena!"

It was true that Whitson regarded his Florentine residence in the light of a political exile. He liked to consider himself as the Tory minister to a brownstone queen who had been hounded from office by a cabal of radicals, impatient of law and order. For the noble program that he had tried to institute had been nothing less than to establish the ground rules for New York society: what families were to form its base; how new ones were to be admitted; what events should be considered primary; what clubs should be favored; even what clothes and decorations should be worn and on what occasions. He had organized a group of ladies, under the leadership of Euphemia Slocum, to give his doctrine the force of law. And for a few years it had looked as if he might actually succeed.

It still, as late as 1923, seemed to him a lofty ideal. Why should the biggest city of the New World, the leading commercial metropolis of the globe, not have an ordered and dignified oligarchy to set the pace in manners and morals, in the beautification of life, in the encouragement of the arts and in the establishment of a style of living that would offer a fitting reward for the successful? Was this not preferable to the alternative of a vulgar mob of crude speculators with fat, bejeweled spouses, pushing their way in everywhere, building crazy gingerbread castles and making themselves contemptible to European eyes? Well, that was what New York society had become. And yet there were people who seemed content with this, people who regarded Whitson as a dreamer, a fusspot, an old maid, an ass. Such was the fate of any American male who dared concern himself with aught but the making of money.

It was only after the war that Whitson had become a friend of Bernard Berenson. Of course, they had often met, and the diminutive but dapper art connoisseur with the grave, beautiful eyes had treated the older man with his invariable quiet courtesy and charm, but there had been little in Whitson's story to arouse more than Berenson's mild amusement. "B.B." enjoyed gossip about the expatriate community, and Whitson always had a succulent anecdote for him. But it was not until the hierophant of the Italian Renaissance had read the novels of Alistair Temple, at the urging of his friend Edith Wharton, and discovered the intimate connection between Whitson and Temple, that his real curiosity was aroused.

"I had not known, my friend," Berenson told Whitson at a tea party in Fiesole, "that you were acquainted with that great genius of American letters. I have recently been reading his exquisite *Paradise to Come*. To have written that at forty-five, and then have simply died! Think of it. But perhaps he had done his thing, had told his tale. Perhaps three novels were all we were to have had, like the seven masterpieces of Pisanello."

"You really rank Temple that high?" Whitson asked in surprise. "His books were not so well esteemed when they were published. I thought people generally found him prolix and obscure."

"He was, perhaps, ahead of his time. What was he like?"

Whitson gazed thoughtfully from the terrace where they were standing down over the cascading vineyards of the hillside. Then he glanced across to the brown panorama of Florence.

"He was damp," he said at last.

"Damp?"

"Moist. He had thick, black, glossy hair that seemed wet and big, brown, watery eyes. He had a way of standing too close to you and looking at you gravely as he uttered some absurdly flattering remark. And I'm afraid he had bad breath."

"Dear me! I thought they hated that in America. You mean he wasn't a social success?"

"He was a good deal taken up by certain families on the fringe of society. But no doubt I am prejudiced. He treated me badly. In fact, he was a kind of Benedict Arnold. I refer to a traitor in our revolutionary war."

"You forget, my friend, that I, too, am American."

"I'm sorry, B.B.! You always strike me as belonging to all nations."

The mild motion of Berenson's hand waived the apology. But his curiosity about Temple was evidently strong enough to make him persistent. He now actually offered himself as a guide for a morning's tour of the Uffizi and as a host for luncheon afterwards if Whitson would agree to discuss his former friend. Whitson hesitated. He well knew the value of such a bid.

"Could we make it the Pitti?"

Berenson seemed amused. "You regard that as the superior collection?"

"It has more portraits."

"Ah, it is the art of representing the physiognomy that you prefer?"

Whitson decided to be bold. He knew that the great man was laughing at him, but he didn't care. Information was what he was after, and this was his chance. Berenson would never make such an offer twice.

"I like portraits of princes. Of peers. Of great people."

"You are concerned with the mystery of power! Good, my friend. I like a man to know what he is after in art. The Pitti is just the place for us."

They spent two hours there the very next morning. Berenson descanted fascinatingly on the intrigues and ambitions of the Medici, the Strozzi, the Orsini, before their bejeweled and bedizened likenesses. Whitson knew enough to keep quiet. But when they had paused for several minutes before a portrait of a woman by Pontormo about which the great critic seemed to have no comment, he ventured at last to ask who the subject was.

"We do not know, other than that she was a lady of the highest rank."

"How can you tell that?"

Berenson gave him an inscrutable look. "Because, for perhaps the first time in Florentine painting, the artist seems more concerned with rendering his sitter's social position than her personality."

"Perhaps her personality *was* her social position."

"My friend, you are profound. But it still marks the beginning of modern vulgarity."

At luncheon, at a carefully chosen restaurant, on a terrace with a view of the Palazzo Vecchio, Berenson was silent as he ate his spaghetti. He chewed each mouthful for a good two minutes, took a long sip of Chianti, and then wiped his lips carefully with the napkin secured under his collar. When he spoke at last, it was to ask his guest gravely what he expected to glean from the Florentine portraitists. Whitson leaned forward eagerly in his chair.

"I want to find out why painters and sculptors who made their reputations by illustrating the lives of the rich and powerful are adored in Florence and despised in New York!" As B.B. simply stared at him, perhaps even wonderingly, Whitson continued emphatically: "Michelangelo could turn an idiotic syphilitic duke of Urbino into a glorious brooding warrior, and everyone shrieked in acclaim. But if Sargent transformed some bosomy Mrs. Stuyvesant into a splendid Clytemnestra, people called him a society sycophant. Why are the feasts of the Medici great pageants and the balls of the Vanderbilts only ostentation?"

"May we not simply suppose that the earlier era produced the greater geniuses?"

"But why is the artist whose subject is society any better than that society?"

"Better?"

"Profounder. Deeper. More estimable."

"Because he must see it in a different light. He illuminates it."

"Ah, but *does* he? Because he pretends to spoof it or satirize it or condemn it? Could he do any of those things if he weren't basically fascinated by it? As much so as the crudest social climber? Didn't Rigaud and Nattier adore their princes and princesses? Didn't Thackeray and Proust — and doesn't even your friend Mrs. Wharton — fundamentally make love to the society they pretended to criticize?"

Berenson now abruptly united their interests. "Is Alistair Temple the artist you are thinking about? Did *he* care about society?"

"To his dying gasp! There never was such an ardent climber!"

"And that is why you resent his great reputation?"

"Yes! Alistair Temple has passed into legend as a genius, while I remain a silly ass. Why? Because he amused himself by pushing his way into society and then making fun of it, while I was breaking my foolish heart to give it some kind of dignity? Because he was sneering while I was building? Yet *he* is called the creator!"

It was May, and the air on the restaurant terrace was velvety. Berenson raised his eyes to the dome of the cathedral appearing over the block across the way and seemed to reflect.

"I think this may be the moment for you to tell me about Temple," he suggested. "You have finished your meal. I am sorry to be so slow at eating, but it will give you the chance to talk without interruption."

Whitson's agitation began to settle as he looked back in memory on his old betrayal, and after a few moments he was calm enough. Berenson's detachment was soothing. Whitson began.

"Alistair Temple came of a respectable but undistinguished Brooklyn family. He had inherited a small sum of money whose income might have just sustained a bachelor of modest needs in a boarding house. But he chose instead to blow it. He figured it would last him three years. He called on me at the Patroons Club, where I then lived, on the strength of a letter from an uncle of his who had been my Columbia classmate, and, in perfect seriousness, expounded his plan. He wanted to 'be in society' for the period that his money would afford him the proper clothes and lodging and the means of traveling to the grandest country houses.

"'And what do you propose to do when your money is gone, young man?' I asked him in astonishment, for his disregard in this respect shocked me even more than his assumption that he could get into society.

"'Oh, I shall let fate take care of that. How many people know what they want today, let alone tomorrow? I at least am very firm about what I want today.'"

"I like that," Berenson intervened, nodding. "I like a young man to have a plan. And he attached himself to you, did he? He became your disciple in the task of reforming society?"

"Precisely. I even found myself becoming very fond of him. He was a kind of adopted nephew. He glided swiftly enough through every door that I opened for him, but he always looked back respectfully to show me that he knew to whom he owed it. And his manners were good, if a bit unctuous. There was sympathy in his dark brown eyes that made him attractive to older women. He had a proper respect for detail. He would call on me every morning at my club to help me with my plans, like a good secretary. He was patient, industrious, accurate. There were moments, I admit, when I suspected that he might be smiling at me, smiling perhaps at my whole world, but I thought at least it was a kindly smile."

"And it wasn't?"

Whitson became very grave at this. "B.B., the man was simply planning treason!"

"You mean he was going to 'write you up'?"

"No. I will not say that I ever found myself pilloried in his novels, though, mind you, I had a hard time getting through them. He might have assassinated my character, I suppose, in one of those interminable paragraphs that put me to sleep. But no, I do not accuse him of using people as models. Unless, of course, they're not recognizable!"

"He was too good a writer for that."

"You think him a great novelist." Whitson shrugged. "Very well. Let us concede it. Personally, I don't think there's a live man or woman in any of his books. Dressmaker's models, that's all. But pass that. What Temple did was something much worse than making sport of me. He destroyed my work! He aborted my great scheme for society. And he did so deliberately, fiendishly, for no purpose other than his own amusement!"

Berenson's gaze was serene. "You mean he constructed a scenario for his own inspiration? He modeled a plot out of real life? And then never used it? How interesting. Perhaps you provided the scaffolding, my friend, which he had later to remove."

"Or the poor old tarpaulin that he yanked off his completed statue," Whitson retorted with a snort. "That would be more like it."

"Tell me what he did."

"It was at the time of the great Smedley ball. Mrs. Ezra

Smedley was a very determined woman. She had commissioned a great palace by Hunt on Fifth Avenue — you remember it, B.B., it was a copy of Azay-le-Rideau . . . ?"

"Ah, yes. And she's since become a collector. She bought that false Mantegna from Prince Loredan."

"And sued him about it. She's not even a good sport. But anyway. She was determined to take New York society by storm. With her great housewarming, a costume ball. I knew Mrs. Smedley and even rather liked her. She had spirit and wit. But it wasn't her time yet. She needed a couple more years of polishing. A few more snubs. There could be no idea of Mrs. Smedley inviting Mrs. Slocum to her ball, as the latter had never called on her, and I advised Mrs. Slocum not to do so until the ball was over and we had had a chance to assess its success. My illustrious patroness seemed to be entirely of my persuasion. Until events took an unfortunate turn. It appeared that her daughter, Miss Abigail Slocum, without my approval had been secretly rehearsing a quadrille for the Smedley ball and had set her heart on performing it. Mrs. Smedley discovered this and saw her chance. She let it be known, by sundry remarks dropped in sundry places, that she regretted that Miss Slocum's artistic efforts were being thrown away. For how could she possibly send a card for her ball to a young lady whose mother had never called on her?"

"Blackmail." Berenson touched his fingertips together. "Surely the great Mrs. Slocum did not stoop to pay the ransom."

"B.B., you don't know what such women are! Under the stiff stance, the whalebone, the eagle eye, the glittering parure, there often beats the heart of a craven. Mrs. Slocum was afraid of the world, afraid of criticism, afraid of her own daughter. Afraid of everyone, I suppose, but my own poor self. She agreed with all my arguments about standing fast and promised to be guided by them. But she nevertheless slipped off in her carriage to leave her card at Azay-le-Rideau. How Eliza Smedley's heart must have quickened as she watched from behind the curtains of her parlor the maroon-coated equerry delivering that fatal bit of pasteboard to her impassive butler on the stoop below! New York society — or should I say the *hope* for a New York society — simply fell to pieces at that moment!"

"I see." Berenson shook his head. "Had Marc Antony not been drunk the night before Philippi, had Cleopatra's nose been a half-inch longer — our fate, dear Worthington, depends on such trivia. But how did Temple come into it?"

"He was the engineer. It was he who organized that wretched quadrille. It was he who induced the uninvited Miss Slocum to take part in it. And it was he who put the idea in Mrs. Smedley's head of what use she might make of it!"

"Because she bribed him?"

"No! Maybe. It doesn't matter. He did it because he wanted to divert himself by creating a drama in New York society. A great drama!"

"How do you know that?"

"He told me so! He had the inimitable gall to throw it in my very face when I accused him of betraying me. He even went so far as to say that he had thought *I* might be amused by it, too."

"And you were not." Berenson shook his head sadly. "No, I am sure you were not. And did his little game really affect your position as arbiter of New York society?"

"It simply ruined me. It made me ridiculous. My position had always been precarious. It depended on the preservation of my favor with a single dowager. And Euphemia Slocum cast me off like an old shoe, as soon as she understood that the truth would make her look like a poltroon. I had to pay the price of her panic. It was *she,* she cried to the world, who had decided, against my crabby conservatism, that the time had come for the Smedleys. A great new era had started. Everyone who had been denied Mrs. Slocum's door in the preceding decade now sharpened a knife for my throat. Like President Wilson, I was 'too proud to fight.' I retired to Florence!"

"And Temple? Did he not retire as well?"

"Yes, but only because his money ran out. He went to live with a blind old aunt in Trenton and wrote his three novels."

"Wrote them and died."

"So it seemed."

"And you care for none of them?"

"Well, what is there to care about? What happens in *Paradise to Come*? Nothing at all."

"Exactly. Nothing at all. Or perhaps everything. A young lady of fabulous fortune and ancient lineage is pursued by fortune hunters in New York in the nineties. She evades them all and finally marries a plain, dull, middle-aged gentleman of no particular means. She devotes herself utterly to his happiness." Berenson paused to dramatize his conclusion. "Her reward is to be robbed and deserted!"

"How can you call that 'everything'?" Whitson protested. "It's the stupidest tale ever told. And why would she be rich? Those old families were just as apt to be poor."

"Perhaps Temple was not concerned with social realism. We never really know where Bessie's fortune comes from or even what her family's house is like. We know only that it is very ugly and filled with beautiful things. I think Temple saw the old New York families and the new as basically alike. Both live in the same kind of monstrous edifices where even the finest assemblage of art objects amounts to a clutter."

"Ugly houses and no plot. A most readable book! And what about the characters? *Are* there any? Bessie, the heroine — can you picture her?"

Berenson half-closed his eyes as he again touched his fingertips together. "Not in facial detail, like a lady in a Ghirlandaio portrait. But in the mass, yes, splendid, like a great, pale figure in a

Piero della Francesca. Or perhaps even like one of those large female figures in a white tunic, against a plain red beach or a flat blue sky — a sort of classic background — that Picasso has been doing recently. Grave, unfathomable, awesome, yet strangely moving. We see Bessie only in her effect on others. That is the magic of Temple's glorious tapestry of prose. The mercenary characters, the 'poor' ones, glint like gold in the dark, while she encompasses them in a kind of cerulean sky. It is as if riches in New York were being equated with virtue, and poverty with vice. Why? I don't profess to know. There may be some kind of allegory there, or myth. All I'm sure of is that I am touched to the heart with a pervading sense of Bessie's beauty of soul." He sighed. "I find reading Temple a unique aesthetic experience."

"But was *his* soul beautiful?"

"You must distinguish, my friend, between an artist's individual personality and his artistic one. The former has little to do with his art. Shakespeare is supposed to have been a lovable man; Wagner is known to have been often hateful. The matter is irrelevant to *Hamlet* and *Tristan*. The artistic personality is the creator. And that is something totally detached from the vulgar appetites, from greed, from Mammon, from snobbishness and social ambition. Alistair Temple the man may have been everything you think. But Alistair Temple the artist had not the smallest ounce of worldliness. Of that I am convinced."

They had finished their meal now, and together they commenced a slow stroll across the Piazza della Republica. Berenson had taken a crust of bread with him, and he proceeded to scatter crumbs for the pigeons. Whitson watched him uneasily.

"So you really think, B.B., that I have known one great artist?"

"I do."

"And can I claim, do you think, that I helped him? That I provided him with raw material? I should like to think that my existence has not been totally useless."

"Who knows?" Berenson stood still for a moment and let his eyelids droop. "Perhaps your brave vision of yourself as the architect of a reconstituted society was the seed of his portrait of Bessie!"

"Are you laughing at me?"

Berenson's eyes opened with a snap. "Yes!" he exclaimed, with something like impatience, and headed to where his limousine was waiting.

The Cup of Coffee

THE WORLD IS COMPOSED of two kinds of people: those who want things badly enough to sacrifice human dignity to obtain them, and those who do not.

I suppose that the incident between Denis Crater and myself brought out one of the basic questions of our time: was my throwing up my job in his company the simple preservation of a minimal integrity, or was it a hysterical act of self-exhibitionism? My children think the former; my wife, the latter. I believe that it was simply a happy chance — a chance that operated as the catharsis of an ancient apprehension.

For right up to the day of my supposedly quixotic decision, I was never what I seemed to be. Who is? I seemed prosperous, complacent, stuffy, a typical 1970 organization man. I was an executive vice-president of Arco Home Appliances, with headquarters at Armonk. I had a house with a three-car garage and a swimming pool at New Canaan. I was an Episcopalian and played golf. Can't you see me? And, yes, I had a boy, Freddy, at Yale, who wanted to be a professional guitarist, and a daughter, Alice, at N.Y.U., who wanted to blow up the world. I had come to accept their affectionate contempt as all a father could ask. I had even decided that it might be the proper role of the husband-spouse of the suburbs to act as a foil, to make his son feel like Segovia, his daughter like Emma Goldman, and his wife... well, to make Matilda feel that she was alive.

But, of course, underneath I seethed with anxiety. Again, who doesn't? I was constantly afraid that I would lose my job, my wife, my little pile of stocks and bonds. When I went to the doctor for my annual checkup I was convinced that he would find a symptom of cancer, and when I went up in a plane I was sure it would crash. But in addition to these perfectly normal reactions, I was haunted by the fear that I would show my fear. I was scared pink of looking pink. I always perfectly understood the man in my squadron in World War II who tried to jump out of a bomber in a raid over Berlin. He preferred death to the fear of death. And I suppose the reason that I could never understand why the people around me saw me as so different from my own image of myself — saw me, indeed, as a pompous, self-confident ass — was that a lifetime's effort to cover my fear had succeeded.

The terrible thing about Denis Crater was that he seemed to have penetrated my disguise. I thought I could make this out in his leer down the table in board meetings, in his sly, friendly, mocking questions. I thought I could make it out in the falsely protecting arm that he placed about my shoulder if we walked down a corridor together. Denis was like a wet, blustering natural disaster given an ironic female name by hydrographic officers, a flood that drenched without enriching, that blew without cooling, that destroyed without cleansing. It had taken only one of his huffs and puffs to engulf my little Arco Home Appliances in the damp embrace of his amalgamated empire. Oh, these mergers! That a man could wake up in New Canaan, free, happy and seemingly secure, and drive over to Armonk to discover that he was as much a slave as a Goth in the court of Caligula!

I suppose that Denis Crater had come to think of himself as a kind of god. He made royal progresses to his various corporations, accompanied by a little permanent suite of yes men. He was a fine-looking man, I admit, for seventy, big and bony and bald, very Caesarish, and he had a habit of tossing his arms about as he talked of his abiding affection for the human material in his employ, dropping such phrases as "How blessed I am in my friends!" or "What have I done to deserve so much *fun* out of life?" Of course, it was all part of a public relations act in which he had come to believe and of which perhaps an essential part was the universally recognized obverse side of the coin: his total ruthlessness. At his immense birthday parties you could hear the wives of minor officers murmur with squeals of almost sexual pleasure: "Isn't he marvelous? Of course, he doesn't mean a word of it. He'd give you the sack if it would net him two bucks!"

But to the point. Crater had a little personal habit that fairly mesmerized the officers of his subsidiary corporations. It was a habit that seemed unconscious but that was almost certainly not so. And one that nobody ever mentioned. For even to have whispered it might have been to admit a personal inferiority to one's boss that was hardly decent in a land once visited by the rays of the American dream. The little habit was this: At staff meetings, which were largely taken up by Crater's harangues urging us to redouble our efforts and remold ourselves in the image of our great chairman, coffee was always served. Crater would drink half a cup, almost at a gulp, and then, when the waiter with the Silex approached with a refill, he would dispose of his slops by dumping them into the cup of his nearest neighbor.

Sometimes the neighbor's cup was already empty and could contain the fresh infusion without overflowing. Sometimes it was half-full, so that the boss's unwanted residue would cause a cascade into the saucer. And sometimes the neighbor's cup was still replete, and the little operation resulted in a messy spill onto the tablecloth. But whether Crater's rejected coffee was contained in its new receptacle or caused a degree of flooding, the expression of the proprietor of the abused vessel invariably retained the same impassivity. It never betrayed by so much as a twitch of the muscles or a glance downward that anything untoward had been noted.

I was hypnotized by this little ritual. Was it a despot's reminder of absolute power, the kicking of a faithful dog, or was it a demonstration of trust and affection, like Napoleon's tweaking the nose or pulling the ear of a favored dragoon? I always avoided the seat next to Crater. I even dared to come late to meetings, rushing in with an armful of papers as if I had been detained by a customer and slipping into an empty chair against the wall. And I always shook my head at the waiter with the coffee Silex so that I would not have a cup available in case the great man, rising and circling the table as he talked, should happen to carry his cup with him and feel the sudden need of a hot refill as he passed my chair. Sometimes I thought he noticed my maneuvers. Sometimes it seemed to me that I caught the flash of humor in those large opaque eyes, a kind of threat that my turn was coming.

And of course it did.

"No, no, Tommy Trimbolt, you're not slipping down to the end of the table today. I have reserved thee this empty chair beside me. Sit down, my friend, sit down. Sit down and elucidate us on why it was necessary to take eighteen thousand more square feet on Lydecker Street *after* I had canceled the Schwartz dryer sale. Of course, I realize that there must be an answer . . . no, no, my dear Tommy, you needn't go to the Silex. We have your steaming coffee right here waiting for thee."

Go to the Silex? I had made no such move. Explain the Lydecker lease? I had already explained it. I sat down beside Crater and began haltingly to repeat my explanation, but I could not look at him. I stared down at my papers and mumbled my words, and all the while, out of the corner of my eye, I watched the hot, brimming cup of coffee at my side.

"Okay, Tommy, okay. That seems to answer the question.

Shall we proceed to Jerry O'Brien's report? Oh, waiter! Some more coffee here."

No condemned criminal can have watched the masked headsman approach him on the scaffold with more dread than I watched the waiter with the Silex move forward in response to Crater's nod. Hypnotized, even though knowing the unspoken rule that one should avert one's eyes from the deed, I now frankly stared at the long, gray, hairless hand of my boss as it moved to his cup. I saw the fingers with dirty nails raise it and approach a point above my own. The brown, creamy substance cascaded into my cup, flooding it, flooding the saucer, and causing a wide, shameful stain on the tablecloth. I looked up at Crater and smiled.

That was on a Monday morning. On Friday night, when I got home, I knew by Matilda's meeting me in the front hall that something had happened. She was holding a copy of the picture magazine *See*.

"Have you read this?"

"Not yet. Does it have the profile of Crater?"

"It does."

"I don't suppose *I'm* mentioned."

"Oh, but you are."

Matilda's angular features, her pale, white, dead skin, her sandy, bobbed hair, her long, pointed nose, seemed all to coalesce, for the first time, into something almost formidable, something that appeared to be calling for an account. She had always had a faintly Tudor look, but the spirit that might have been expected to lurk behind that cool mask had hitherto been curiously absent. Matilda was a woman of long silences, of strange inertias. It had been possible for us to be married for twenty-five years with almost no confrontations. She had a rather graceful way of accepting our lack of communion as if it were the common lot. Or had had.

"Let me see."

I sat on the hall bench and read the article. It was written by a radical journalist who had carried little but his bad manners from the Greenwich Village rag in which he had made his name to the big illustrated weekly in which he hoped to make his fortune. He had a lot of obvious fun with the arrogance of Denis Crater, yet his piece was still infused with an admiration that struck me as being as basic as that of any of the latter's vice-presidents. He must have been present at the Monday board meeting, for the little episode of the coffee slops was related in full: "Executive Vice-President Thomas Trimbolt surveyed sadly the creamy, cold bilge into which his steaming black brew had been converted. Like Job, he had no complaints. God had spoken. That was all."

I laughed. "How true."

Matilda nodded, and I noted that not for a moment had she questioned the accuracy of the story. Oh, she knew her man! But perhaps not quite as well as she imagined.

"The children are here," she said grimly. "Freddy drove over from New Haven, and Alice came up from N.Y.U. They're both very upset. They can't believe you'd put up with such insulting conduct."

"I thought it was precisely what they could believe."

"You're their father, after all." Never had I seen Matilda so intense, so organized. Mother love had evidently galvanized her into unexampled activity. "And I've figured it out. Here's what you must tell them. Say that before Mr. Crater did what he did, he asked you, in a voice that the reporter couldn't catch, if you were going to drink your coffee."

"And I told him I was!" I exclaimed with a shout of laughter.

"Tommy, this is serious. Your children have become laughing-stocks in their colleges."

"Let us talk to them," I said, rising. Decidedly, I was enjoying myself.

They were playing records in the living room, but as a token of the gravity of the occasion Freddy turned the machine off. He was big, blond, hulking, hirsute, helpless, with the mildest blue eyes I had ever known. It struck me at once that these eyes were looking at me for the first time. Not so Alice's. *She* had seen me before. She was a militant protester of all the usual things, broad-browed, thin-lipped, straight-haired, with female vanity manifest in the perfect fit of her blue jeans and in her balletlike movements.

"Your father has a perfectly good explanation," Matilda blurted out. "He never touches coffee, and Mr. Crater knows it."

"But I always ask for a fresh cup so he can use it for his slops."

"Tommy, I warn you!" Matilda cried harshly.

"It's a kind of ritual," I explained. "I present the backside, and he presents the kick. Like the priest and the fatted calf. Does either really have a choice?"

"Dad, listen." Freddy strode up and down the carpet, his big hands pushed into his small hip pockets. "This is really rough. At lunch today five guys filed by my table and dumped coffee in my cup. I took a poke at one of them, and the place was in an uproar."

"He may not get into a fraternity!" Matilda exclaimed.

"Oh, Ma!" Alice cried in disgust. "Freddy doesn't care about that. Freddy and I simply object to having a name that has become overnight a symbol of obeisance to the establishment. A trademark of the fawning attitude of organization men to economic barbarians! We want to know what Dad is going to do about it."

"What *can* I do about it, Alice?"

"You can announce to the press that you will no longer work for such a boor. You can resign."

"And who will support you?"

"That's a detail. We'll get along."

This, I had to concede, was true. At least so far as Alice was concerned. The young are not worldly.

"But your mother and I might not," I pointed out. "There are too many things we want. The world is divided into two kinds of people, Alice. Those who want things and those who don't. If you want something badly enough, you will forget dignity. If you don't, you won't."

"Oh, Dad, do you really think the world is made up entirely of little company back-stabbers in gray suits? There are bigger people. I know some!"

"Only if they don't want anything," I insisted. "And I'm not confining myself to little company back-stabbers. No, indeed, I'm talking about big people. As big as you want. Your great statesman has to pander to the mob to win an election. Your great soldier has to smirk and flatter to get a command. Even in love it's so. Won't the true lover submit to humiliation? You'll find out all about it someday, Alice. You'll meet some bearded, leather-jacketed bully who'll strike you as possessing the political keys of the future, and you'll do anything for him."

"Tommy!" my wife warned me again.

"She will, Matilda! And when you want something badly enough, fawning becomes noble. It becomes sacrifice."

"No!" both children cried.

"You can't face the world," I told them, shaking my head. "You can't face the world as it is." Then I paused as a sudden thought struck me. "Perhaps nobody can. Perhaps, really, nobody can."

"Surely Mr. Crater can," Alice said sneeringly.

"Oh, he least of all."

Freddy turned on me now with unconcealed disgust. "But even if what you say is true, how can you care enough about getting ahead in household appliances to put up with a gorilla like Crater?"

And then a funny thing happened to me. I realized that I didn't care enough. I realized that I didn't give a damn. I had only cared that what had happened should not have happened.

"Maybe you're right, Freddy!" I exclaimed. "Maybe I've always had myself wrong. Maybe, after all, *I* belong to those who don't want things." I looked bemusedly about at these three strangers who constituted my family. "Whereas you three are all wanters. Yes! I see it. Matilda, you want your children's love. Of course you do. There's nothing in the world you wouldn't do to keep it. And Freddy wants to be respected by his pals at Yale. He'd give anything to have yesterday's anonymity back. And Alice wants to be able to worship some Weatherman and make bombs. Ah, you poor dear creatures! You all suffer from the pathos of loneliness in an overpopulated world. I pity you. I, who want nothing."

Well, this provoked an uproar. Never before had I taken the offensive with them. We talked till late at night, and by the time we all went to bed I was actually "communicating" with my son and daughter. That is, they had ceased to treat me as a total idiot. Matilda was another matter. She was obviously apprehensive of the contents of the Pandora's box that the children had opened, but what could she do? She had started it, after all.

The next morning, at the office, I was summoned by Mr. Crater.

"My dear fellow," he began, in a peculiarly beneficent tone, as soft and mauve as the curtains that rimmed his cage of glass on the top of our building, "I have news for thee. How would thee like a little sojourn, say for three years, in Topeka? I see you in soap pads. Yes, dear friend, I definitely see you in soap pads. I looked at a memo only this morning that I had jotted down just a year ago. It read, quite simply, 'Trimbolt. Soap pads.' "

"Did it read, 'Trimbolt. Soap pads. Executive vice-president'?"

"No, I do not recall that it did."

"So this, then, is a demotion?"

The opaque eyes were half-concealed by heavy lids. "You might call it that."

"Might thou?"

"I might."

"And might thou tellest me why?"

"I have a little test, Tommy. A little test of executive capacity. It's a very simple trick, but it never fails."

"But we all know it, of course! The coffee slops. The man who sits by while that is done to him cannot be an executive type."

Crater's smile seemed not merely to congratulate me. It was a beaming sun that could afford to illuminate the rulers and the ruled.

"So, my dear fellow, you see!"

"Certainly. But I also see that you haven't an executive in any of your companies. For who has passed your test?"

Crater's smile faded slowly as he found himself in the novel position of having to answer. Then it beamed again as he saw his way. "Well, there you are, dear fellow! None of them has. It's why I can never retire!"

I rose. "That's a good answer, and the one I expected of you. But of course it's all a farce. You adopted the test theory when you read that article in *See*. For you cannot face the facts. You cannot bear to live in a world where a man will deliberately cringe, yea, fawn and prostrate himself, before such a thing as Denis Crater. I hardly blame you. It's a funny world. But I see it."

Crater's voice was even silkier. "My dear fellow, I begin to wonder if I even see thee in soap pads."

"Oh, of course I'm quitting. I only came around this morning to see if I could call you a son of a bitch without experiencing the least titillation, the least pleasure. Simply as a matter of course. I find that I can."

Crater ran around the desk to grip my shoulders. "Tommy boy, I love you. Stay with me! Succeed me!"

But I did not even smile as I shook myself loose and strode from the room. He bored me. That was all.

The Cruise

WHEN BETTY LAMB lost her husband, she was seventy-one and had been married for forty-five years. Fred had been several years older, and his decline had been long and agonizing. At the end, thoroughly depleted, Betty primarily felt relief; nobody with a heart could have wished a further protraction of that suffering, senile state. Yet she nonetheless felt that without him, even without the poor shriveled hulk that this once fine man had become, she was only an empty sack.

It was certainly not that she lacked advantages. She seemed if anything unduly blessed. Her health was excellent; her three happily married and profitably employed children, devoted; her income, more than adequate to support her in her comfortable Riverside Drive apartment and to take her occasionally to Europe. The trouble was that there was nothing she wanted to do.

"It's not that I'm really unhappy," she explained to Timothy, the oldest and most concerned of her children. "Or even that I want very much to die. It's simply that I've lost my taste for life. I feel that I've accomplished whatever it was I was meant to accomplish here. I've had a good time — a very good time — but I've had enough, that's the point. Oh, darling, don't look so worried! You're not going to have to count my sleeping pills or bar my windows. I'm not going to do anything that would upset or embarrass any of you children. I shall live out my life quite patiently, as long as I must. I hope it's not too long, that's all. And I'm afraid it will be. Dr. Requa says I'm as strong as the proverbial horse."

"And thank God for that!" Timothy exclaimed warmly. "We'll teach you there's lots left in life. You'll see."

Timothy, who played tennis every evening and jogged on weekends in Central Park, had a touching faith in the diversions of the modern world. He was never at a loss for a suggestion to occupy his mother's ballooning leisure time: bridge or canasta lessons, debating classes, painting, découpage, concert series, even a course in wine-tasting. His countenance became very grave when Betty smilingly accused him of turning life into a game.

"Life may be a game," he cautioned her. "But that's no reason not to play it. I think you should take a cruise."

Betty had been determined to avoid that most sacred of diversions of the old and well-to-do, but Timothy was inflexible.

"It's so absurd," she protested. "This idea that there's something actually meritorious in travel! As if a succession of images of ports and palaces across elderly eyeballs, plus a thousand rubbers of bridge, could provide any real benefit to the mind or soul!"

"You get a change of climate and a change of air," Timothy insisted. "You meet new people. And how can you be so set against something you've never done?"

As the other children concurred with Timothy, she at length agreed to book herself on a cruise, if only to prove to them that she wouldn't like it. She selected one that went from New York to Rio, Casablanca and Naples, in order to have the maximum of blue water and the minimum of bazaars.

It started out as badly as she had feared. In Antigua she watched in dismay as the passengers, at least half of whom were widows of her vintage, descended on the stores like humanized locusts in a Walt Disney cartoon leaving rifled or empty counters behind them. At sea again, en route to Rio, three friendly ladies asked her to make a regular fourth at their card table, but frightened her off by suggesting that they start the first rubber at eight A.M. And at her table in the dining room, two terrible men, who seemed to have belonged to the New Jersey Mafia, alternated in manner between a precious politeness that repelled her and a sultry surliness that alarmed.

But when the great vessel started eastward on its long trek across the Atlantic and the daily routine was uninterrupted by further prospect of shore excursions, she began at last to sense some of the drugged charm of the relentless regularity. Life on board was shielded from all the bogies of home. There was no poverty to reproach one, no jeering youth, no jarring newspapers, no strikes, no communists, no crime. It was like being in a hospital without having to be sick.

And then one day she made two friends, Ned and Roseanne Foxen. He was a fine tall man, a little over seventy, with curly steel-gray hair, smiling blue eyes and a long, thin, handsome face. He wore beautiful tweeds, of rather loud colors, and played all the deck games with great dexterity. He could easily have been the most popular man on board had it not been for his touching solicitude for his ailing wife and his desire to keep her apart from the tiring crush of their fellow passengers. He seemed to have sensed that Betty would be just the right companion for Roseanne when he was doing his rounds of the deck or playing Ping-Pong. But when he was not exercising, he was always with them.

Roseanne Foxen was a quiet, pale, emaciated woman, with large, sad, dark eyes. She made no secret of the fact that her heart condition might finish her off at any moment.

"You get used to anything," she told Betty. "I don't find it too difficult anymore to live from day to day. It can even fill life with a rather bracing intensity. I look forward to soup and crackers at eleven! I like the bingo. It's all very silly, but then, what isn't? One learns not to waste a scrap of life. The only thing that worries me is Ned. I don't quite make out how he is going to get on without me."

"Anyone can see that he adores you. But he strikes me as very strong. As a man who can survive things. Perhaps even loneliness."

"Unlike you, dear." Roseanne reached her long, thin, cold hand from her deck chair to rest it for a moment on Betty's. They had already talked of Betty's listlessness. "Oh, I know he's a survivor. I'm even sure that he'll marry again. What I mean by his not getting on without me is that he needs me for a very particular purpose. I wonder if you can guess what I mean."

Betty thought a moment. She knew that she had to be truthful with this new friend. "Do you perhaps mean that you supply him with balance?"

"Precisely! I keep him from going over the edge."

For Betty had already discovered that Ned Foxen was full of what her late husband would have called "crazy ideas." He believed that Franklin D. Roosevelt had secretly encouraged the Japanese to attack Pearl Harbor in order to involve us in war with Hitler, and that he had then "sold out" to Stalin in Yalta to help the communist cause. He was convinced that John F. Kennedy had been assassinated at the express command of Castro and that Dean Acheson had sent state secrets to Moscow through Alger Hiss. He was always talking about a sinister group called "they" who had infiltrated the American body politic so that at a nod from the Soviet dictator we could expect our whole social fabric to crumble, leaving not a wrack behind.

But what was surprising about Ned was that he manifested none of the choleric indignation or sputtering resentment of the usual type of anti-Red alarmist. He was benign, pleasant, almost cheerful in his acceptance of inevitable doom. He seemed to face the end of Western civilization, or at least the end of Western capitalism, as easily as he would a velvet spring evening after a mild sunny day.

"But he has such charm, Roseanne," Betty offered now as reassurance. "He is always going to appeal to some nice woman's instinct to help him."

"Ah, but will it always be a nice one?"

The Foxens, like most of the passengers, lived in the past. But it was not, Betty noted, necessarily the real past. It was rather a past that was being constantly edited, smoothed, brightened, touched up. It was a past studded with the little victories of the person who was in the process of creating it. Ned Foxen loved to relate to her how cleverly he had dealt with this or that ornery customer of his Buick agency in Rochester and how he had steered a bill to passage in the Albany assembly by playing both sides against the middle. And Roseanne enjoyed telling her how often she had been right in warning her married children not to do the things that they had then done and later regretted. The past had been purged of thorns and bitterness; it was now an unending source of complacency.

And the future? Well, of course, there was not so very much of that to look forward to. It was better to divide one's time between a semifictional past and an artificial present. The world of the cruise was a world that had abolished all the bogies of old people: the difficulty of cooking and cleaning without servants, the problem of how to use leisure time, the ache of loneliness. On board the *Stella Maris,* obsequious Italian stewards administered to their every need; their working hours were filled with a gentle round of cocktail parties, card parties, lectures, movies and deck games; and there was no end of ears in which to plant their reminiscences, no end of tongues to offer them those of others. It was a world in which the only imaginable task was that of mixing the drinks oneself if one entertained in one's cabin.

Even death, if it came on the cruise, was easy. There were several fine coffins, inlaid with satin, ready for emergency, in the hold.

In Naples an excursion to Rome by bus was offered, with two nights in the Eternal City. Roseanne was too ill to go, but she urged her new friend to keep Ned company, and Betty found him an excellent guide, at least where the ancient empire was concerned, for it seemed that he had made a hobby of Latin history. He took her not to the Forum, which, according to him, was only a "ruin" and a "shambles," but to the Museum of Roman Civilization, which was the only place, he claimed, where one could get any real sense of what it might have been like to have lived under Tiberius Caesar or Marcus Aurelius. Standing by a railing to look down on the immense diorama of the capital of the world under Constantine, he waxed almost lyrical.

"Gibbon said that the era of the Antonines was the greatest in history. That was more than a century before what you see here, but the city was probably not too different. They didn't destroy their landmarks the way we do. The quality of life then was something that our benighted souls probably can't even conceive. Imagine the beauty and order, the simple human dignity of it all!"

Betty looked with surprise at his fine clear brow, his gentle, smiling blue eyes. Was there a Roman calm behind that stalwart pose? Did she have a glimpse of the classic simplicity of white temples and blue seas and red rocks? "What about all those poor people who were fed to the lions?" she asked.

"Every civilization has its dark corners." He shrugged. "They had to do something to keep the mob happy."

"And what about the slaves? Weren't there millions of them?"

"Undoubtedly. But they had a definite status in society. They weren't like slaves in our Old South. There was no racial barrier, and they weren't kept illiterate. Some Greek slaves became great philosophers. There were even slaves who advised and dominated emperors!"

Betty reflected that he was probably making a romantic novel out of history, in the way that the cruise made a romantic novel out of life. Yet it was still fun. She wanted to learn more about Ned's Roman Empire. But alas, when they got back to the *Stella Maris*, they found that Roseanne had had a bad heart attack. Ned, very drawn, came out of her cabin to tell Betty that Roseanne wanted to see her alone.

Betty found the room so dark that she could barely make out the long figure on the bunk.

"Can you find the chair, dear?" came her friend's weak voice.

"Certainly." Seated, Betty took the cold hand in hers.

"I'd rather leave the light off, if you don't mind. It makes it easier for me to say what I want to say."

"Oh, I like the dark."

"Do you guess what I want to ask of you?"

"I think so."

"You do, don't you? You're an intuitive woman, Betty. You know that I want you to marry Ned."

"Yes, but I'm not going to. I shall never marry again."

"Ah, don't say that!"

"I must be truthful, dear. Even now. Or rather, particularly now. But I'll do the next best thing. I'll try to see he doesn't fall into the hands of the wrong woman."

"Well, that's fine!"

"That will satisfy you?"

"Yes. Because if you do that, he'll fall into yours! I shall be quite safe."

The door opened a crack. It was the nurse.

"Am I interrupting?"

"Yes!" Betty exclaimed.

"No!" Roseanne said with surprising firmness. "I've said all that I meant to say. Come in, Miss Dunn."

* * *

When Ned Foxen arrived in New York to stay at the Plaza and get "caught up on his operas and plays," only four months after Roseanne's demise, he appeared to have entirely recovered, if indeed his state had been one to be recovered from. He wore no mourning, in his habit or in his demeanor, and he seemed completely natural and easy. He spoke of Roseanne without constraint or embarrassment, as about someone whose great importance in his life and continuing influence could be taken for granted, but who had been dead for a long time. He seemed to take for granted also that Betty would arrange her schedule so as to accompany him to all his plays and operas.

And she did. Except for the fact that he was rather noisily critical of the general inadequacies of waiters, ushers, salesmen and cab drivers, and was constantly comparing the state of the city with its counterpart of thirty years back (a lost metropolis that Betty was beginning to find somewhat mythical), he was, as he had been on the cruise, a most agreeable escort, keeping her amused with his keen interest in all that they heard and saw, or drank and ate. He continued to exhibit the tastes and appetites of a man half his age.

"The *Stella Maris* is going to the Greek islands and Turkey this year," he told her one night at dinner. "It should be a fascinating cruise. We're just beginning to realize the full extent of Roman civilization in Turkey."

"I wonder if I haven't had my fill of Roman civilization."

"Oh, my dear, you're only on the threshold. Just wait."

"You sound as if you thought I was going."

"And so you are!"

Ned insisted on giving a dinner party at an expensive French restaurant for her three children and their spouses. As she feared, her offspring took this almost as a declaration of impending nuptials. They were exhilarated by Ned's wines and his high spirits, and thought him a capital fellow. Timothy, lunching with his mother the next day, was inclined to be absurdly serious about the whole thing.

"But, darling," Betty protested. "Ned and I are simply friends. What on earth do you think you're rushing me into?"

"I'm not rushing you into anything. I'm simply saying that Mr. Foxen is someone who should be considered *if* you should ever want to marry again. He's a prince of a guy. And Billy and Flossie feel just as I do about it."

"So you've been talking us over?" she asked in dismay.

"Of course we've been talking you over. Any idiot can see the man wants to marry you! Isn't it the duty of those who love you and care about you to discuss it?"

"I suppose so." she responded gloomily.

"Now, don't get the idea that anyone's trying to push you into marriage. They're not!"

But they were. Of course they were. They wanted her off their hands, off their minds. They wanted not to have to feel sorry for her. Had she not intruded her woebegone countenance into their fine, fair, bland, desperate, middle-aged lives? Why had she had to tell Timothy that she had lost her taste for life? *That* had been the unforgivable thing. And now they would never be content until she, like a repentant heretic, had donned the fool's cap of recantation and taken her solemn vow that she was serene and interested in life and looking forward to next year's cruise!

Well, she had asked for it. All she had had to do was to have kept her mouth shut, and she had failed. If she ever *should* end up marrying Ned Foxen, as a sheer reparation, it would serve her jolly well right!

But the very next evening, when Ned took her to a nightclub, a couple of small incidents disconcerted her badly. When the cab driver, a Puerto Rican, had to be told where the Primrose-Path was located, Ned explained the directions patiently in Spanish, but then added to Betty in a tone that carried to the front seat: "Another couple of years, and we'll have to tell them how to get to Times Square in Swahili!"

And in the nightclub, when the Italian waiter, bringing her martini and Ned's whiskey sour and being told that the martini was for the lady, asked to whom he should serve the whiskey sour, Ned observed coolly, before the poor fellow had departed: "We can put a man on the moon, but can we teach our worthy immigrants the logic of simple deduction?"

His tone was unimpassioned, his smile even disarming. He seemed to contemplate the human inadequacy about him with an almost benevolent resignation. But there was a condescension in his attitude to what he smilingly described as "the lower orders" that she did not like at all.

"There's something wrong," he said gently, in the middle of their dinner. He had interrupted one of his anecdotes about labor racketeers in Rochester and had been regarding her with a quizzical smile. "You don't approve of me tonight."

"Well, some of your attitudes . . ." She paused, embarrassed. Would he possibly understand? She thought she could not bear to hurt his feelings. He was so kind, so solicitous, and those clear blue eyes seemed almost boyish in their tendered good will. "Some of your attitudes seem the least bit lacking in Christian charity." She hesitated again before his obvious bafflement. "Or should I say Christian love?"

"You mean I don't love people? Betty! You should know better than that."

"Well, on the cruise somehow it seemed different. Maybe it was the sky and the sea, the sheer sparkle of things. If you complained about the service, or about our fellow passengers, or even about the politics of the world . . . well, it was all great fun."

"And it isn't here?"

"No!" She became bolder as she hazarded the emphasis. "When you tell me that Americans are soft and spoiled and hooked on drugs, and that we're bound to go down like ninepins before the Soviets or the Third World . . ." Again she stopped.

"And you don't think we will." He was patient, reasonable, as always.

"Well, I don't think that's somehow the point. The point is that when people talk as you do here, in New York — not on a cruise, that is — it's somehow different. It's . . . well, it's not nice."

"How, not nice?"

"Well, I seem to see people giving up and turning to . . . to a man on a white horse!"

He stared. "And you don't like men on white horses?"

"No, I guess that's just it. I don't like men on white horses."

For a moment their eyes met, and then, easily, affably, he changed the subject. But somehow she knew, with a thrill of relief, and even with a thrill of regret, that now he would never propose to her.

* * *

Betty had thought she would never take another cruise, but she was wrong. She would never take another cruise, it turned out, for her own diversion, but she would take one for somebody else's. When her sister's husband, Sam Dodge, died, Esther, who lived in Greenwich and had always been considered rather too "swell" for the Lambs, now discovered, in the abrupt collapse of her life, that "good old Betty" had more time and even more kindness to offer her than two preoccupied and prosperous married daughters, even though the latter lived on the same road and made much public articulation of filial piety. But Betty was the one who was willing to visit Esther for days at a time and provide a silent and consoling presence and a helpful hand in household chores.

Esther was a smaller, prettier version of her older sister. As girls they had enjoyed comparing themselves to Jo and Amy March in *Little Women*. Betty had purported to see in herself some of the honesty and bluntness of the deeply feeling Jo, while Esther, a bit complacently, had emulated the superior sophistication of the more subtly feminine Amy. And Esther, like her fictional counterpart, had made the greater marriage. Sam Dodge had not only supplied her first with Cadillacs and later with Mercedeses, a Tudor mansion on Round Hill Road and a villa in Barbados; he had also spoiled her, cosseted her, taken her side vigorously at the smallest implied criticism, within the family or without. The obvious fault of this was that it had ensured her a helpless widowhood.

It was Betty who first proposed to Esther the idea of a Caribbean cruise to the Panama Canal Zone. It had occurred to her, watching her sister sitting listlessly in the conservatory, afternoon after afternoon, with an unread copy of *Harper's Bazaar* on her lap, that she might be better off on a deck chair, where her eyes could rest on the sparkling blue of the sea instead of those same static potted plants. Perhaps Esther would prove to be one of those for whom cruises had been invented.

And so it seemed, on the very second day out from New York. Esther insisted that she didn't want to talk to anyone, or even to meet anyone, and Betty carefully shielded her from would-be-friendly fellow passengers. In the morning the sisters sat on their deck chairs; in the afternoon they looked at the movie; in the evening they listened to the ship's concert. They had a table alone in the dining room and drank their cocktails alone in their cabin. By the time the ship dropped anchor in Antigua Esther was showing distinct signs of revival. Instead of talking exclusively about herself, she began now to descant on the inadequate sympathy bestowed upon her by Sam's partners, by Sam's family and even by Sam's daughters.

Ned Foxen, unexpected, joined the cruise at Antigua. He seemed as surprised to see Betty as she to see him. He looked as handsome and shining as ever, and Esther, after peeking at him from her deck chair, consented to be introduced. His tact in promptly taking in her desolate situation was admirable. He made it clear at once that if he were admitted to their company, there would be no danger of further enlargements. Like Betty, he would protect the new widow from an intrusive world.

Esther, charmed by his manner, discussed his proposition with Betty in their cabin. She had always taken men seriously; it was one subject on which she was capable of rising above exclusively personal concerns.

"After all, dear, he's *your* friend. There's no reason on earth you should have a sister in tow all the time. I'm perfectly happy to be left alone in my deck chair any time you want to stroll the deck or play shuffleboard with Mr. Foxen."

"I'm sure you are, dear. But it so happens there's nothing in the least special about me and Ned Foxen. I like him very much, but I shall like him just as much *with* you. Even more, actually. I think it's time you had a change from so steady a diet of older sister."

"But what about him?" Esther demanded in a sharper tone. "What makes you think he wants to be saddled with two widows?"

"Oh, I've no doubt he could take three or four! Why don't we try, anyway? We can always go back to the way we were."

Esther's stare assessed the situation. "All right," she said at last, with a nod. "So long as you're sure."

"I'm sure! I have no monopoly on Ned Foxen. And no desire to have one."

Ned was perfect. He treated the sisters with absolute equality.

When they strolled about the deck, he had one on each arm. When they played cards, it was three-handed bridge — never a question of a fourth. It was a matter of only a couple of days before Esther suggested to Betty that they ask him to join their table in the dining room. From then on they were an inseparable threesome.

Conversation, however, as Betty soon discovered, tended to be more two ways than three. Esther and Ned were immediately congenial in their common concern over modern assaults on order and decorum. Esther, indeed, appeared to derive an actual exhilaration from the cheerful way in which Ned would cap her most dismal tale with a yet more dismal one.

"Have you ever noted a curious thing about our Supreme Court?" Ned's smile, as he helped the ladies to more wine, might have been the accompaniment of some comic or romantic tale. "While it proclaims a passionate concern for the liberty of the individual and warbles about freedom from oppression and fear, it is actually creating a new reign of terror. For who avail themselves of these great new freedoms from an oppressive police state? Peddlers of dope to minors. Racketeers who terrorize the waterfront. Pimps who beat up reluctant prostitutes. Protection merchants who sell their products by murder and mayhem. Oh, I assure you, it's a merry crowd! I hope you ladies have given your annual contribution to the American Civil Liberties Union. Please do! Otherwise some poor Mafioso may have to spend a few weeks in 'durance vile.' "

"That's what I tell my daughters!" Esther exclaimed, clapping her hands. "It's all very well to talk about police brutality, but has anyone who was minding his own business ever been brutalized?"

Betty remembered her revulsion that night at the Primrose-Path. Why was it different now? Was it just the sun and the sea? The discussion between Esther and Ned seemed to her as harmless as the chattering of the gulls in their wake.

Yet that night Betty slept badly. She found her mind suddenly assaulted by a ridiculous dream in which America appeared as simply a source of fortunes, a kind of emerald jungle from which gold and other precious minerals could readily enough be mined, but in which pleasure was precarious and mortal danger constant. The miners, the would-be rich, when not actually engaged in digging, walled themselves up in high pyramids or in country estates surrounded by electrified fences, and when they had at last extracted enough metal from that troubled earth, the only thing they could do with themselves was to put water instead of dirt underneath them and purchase the drugged nirvana of the cruise. But were they not fleeing from death to death? Were Esther and Ned not dead? And were they any more dead than she, Betty, had been at home? And wasn't Ned better off dead than alive as he had been at the Primrose-Path?

The next morning, pale and exhausted, she paced the deck with Ned while Esther was at the hairdresser's.

"May I tell you something, Ned? You have been perfect with my sister." The sea was now as flat and gray as the roof of a garage, and the cloudy sky seemed about to drop upon them. Betty's sense of the vessel as an oasis in an infinite desert was still with her. But she felt, at least, that *her* place was on that slaty horizon. "Esther did not want any company, and I was beginning to be afraid that she was retiring too far from life. It was as if . . ." She hesitated, wondering if her fancy was not becoming a bit ridiculous. But did it really matter? "As if she might float away somehow, off the ship, out there, to all that . . . nothing. But you have helped to peg her here. To tie her down, so to speak."

"She's a wonderful woman, your sister. Deeply sympathetic. And very brave."

"I was beginning to be afraid that she was like me. That she'd lost her attachment to life."

"May I be bold, Betty?" There was a note of unwonted emphasis in Ned's bland tone. "She is not like you. In my opinion Esther has lost none of her attachment to life. She has been momentarily in shock, stunned, if you like. When she recovers, she will recover altogether."

As they rounded the stern and proceeded forward they saw that Esther was back in her deck chair. She waved to them cheerfully, and Betty noted, with a faint surprise, that her hair had been subjected to a blue rinse. Smiling, Betty turned away to let them greet each other alone. She was glad that the cruise was almost over. She preferred the truth of home, if truth it were, to the fantasy of ocean, if fantasy it were.

The Fabbri Tape

I HAVE BEEN FRETTING for some days now over an article in the *Manhattan Law Review*: "Hubris and the American Lawyer," which contains, in addition to essays on Alger Hiss, Dean Landis and John Dean, a piece on myself entitled "Mario Fabbri, Merchant of Justice." Ordinarily, in the now considerable literature dealing with the bribery trial of Gridley Forrest, it is the judge who occupies center stage, and indeed it is hard to imagine a greater exemplar of the arrogance so fatal to the Greek tragic hero than my late, unhappy friend. But this particular author has chosen to see *me* as the principal villain, the mastermind behind the tragedy. And he has taken the trouble to carry his research down to this year of our Lord 1975, for he ends on this note: "Fabbri, hale and hearty at eighty-four, sole survivor of a scandal that four decades ago shook our bar from coast to coast, cheerfully persists in his ancient error. 'Believing what I then believed to be the facts,' he told a reporter recently, 'I'd do the same thing again!'"

It is perfectly true. I would. But it behooves me, I suppose, in an era of general review of moral values, to make some effort to set down my reasons for the benefit of any posterity that cares to hear them. We live in an age of records, where history is transcribed on a minute-to-minute basis. So long as I am still in possession of my faculties, I may as well add my tape to a heap already so high that future scholars will be tempted to make a bonfire of it. Why not? Doesn't each generation want to rewrite history according to its particular lights?

Young people today, including my grandchildren, are very busy reevaluating the morals of the past. They tend to see American history as a study in hypocrisy. To them crime is largely a technical matter. If you are caught, you go to jail, and that is that. You are no longer made an outcast as I was. Unless, of course, you have been guilty of discriminating against an ethnic or religious minority, and then you *are* wicked. Sometimes I think that is the only moral value we have left.

But that is all right. I can live with that. I grew up as a youngster in Manhattan when to be poor, Italian and Catholic was hardly a ticket to fame and riches, and although I always regarded social prejudices as simply hurdles that I had to get over, I can agree that in a decent society they should be eliminated. And as to the concept of other crimes being technically rather than morally reprehensible, I can only point out that that was precisely my own gospel and the reason I did what I did. In an era that valued appearances I strove to save the appearance of the bar, the appearance of the judiciary, indeed the appearance of our whole legal system. I still believe it would have been better for everybody had Gridley Forrest never been found out.

My late wife, I should admit, never agreed with me. She believed that I had been profoundly evil and left me for a time because I would not repent. She would have loved me as a sinner, but only as a repentant sinner. And in the end it was her duty that made her return, not my persuasiveness. She decided that a wife never has the right to give a husband up.

Let me fill in, as briefly as I can, the minimum of background that the person listening to this tape should know. My parents emigrated from Genoa in the late eighteen eighties and started an Italian restaurant in Twelfth Street. I was one of eight children, but because I was bright my father lavished his particular attention on me. His small means required him to pick and choose among his offspring. It was through him that I got a job as an office boy with Mr. Findlay of the great Wall Street law firm that bore his name. Mr. Findlay was a bachelor who lived on Washington Square and frequently dined at my father's place. After my employment he kept a sharp eye on me, and finding me quick, responsive and able, he decided to put me through college and law school and then to hire me as a clerk. Once I had a hand on the bottom rung of that ladder I never loosened my hold. I stayed in the firm until I became a member and, after Mr. Findlay's death in 1930, I succeeded him as managing partner. That is the story, in its very briefest form, of my rise.

Let me say just a word about Thomas Findlay. He was the most impersonal man I have ever known, a close-mouthed, hard-hitting, utterly industrious Yankee. He lived, so far as I could make out, for the love of the law alone. He never spent much money on himself, and he bequeathed the substantial fortune that he made to a hospital in which he had shown only a perfunctory interest in his lifetime. Our relationship was one of symbiosis. As he grew older, he leaned increasingly on me, but he always recognized that I needed him quite as much as he did me. He never praised or dispraised my work. He knew that I knew just how good it was. And somehow, without ever expressing his affection for me, he managed to make me feel it. I was the nearest thing that he had to a son, perhaps the nearest thing to a friend.

The gulf between us, as I look back, seems limitless. He was small and dry and lived to work. I was large and, in my young days, rather floridly handsome, and I craved pleasure as much as work. I loved music and art and food and wine and women.

He did not so much object to these tastes as to seem to find them irrelevant to what life, to him anyway, was all about. The nearest thing we ever had to an intimate conversation was when I told him that I had fallen in love with Pussy Fish, the daughter of one of his partners.

"I suppose it's a social step up for you," he observed, with his usual candor. "But not very far up. And you're quite capable of making it on your own."

"But, Mr. Findlay," I protested, "you don't understand. I love the girl!"

"Of course you do, my boy. I didn't mean to imply the contrary. But girls like that . . . well, they either believe in the things their parents pretend to believe in, or they don't. And I don't know which is worse."

I didn't know what Mr. Findlay meant by that, but it didn't worry me. I was too much in love. I see it now, however. He wondered what would happen to me if I were absorbed into what we now call a WASP culture. Mr. and Mrs. Fish, unlike Mr. Findlay, who had been a poor parson's son from Fitchburg, Massachusetts, were "old New York." Mr. Fish was an elegant, rather wizened, very thin and very brown-faced gentleman who owed his position in the firm to a long deceased father. He had lost his lawyer's nerve (if he had ever had it) and tried to make up for this deficiency by charming manners. He and his rather mousy wife made no objection to my suit for their only daughter; indeed, they seemed to encourage it. After Pussy and I were married, I discovered that they had almost no means besides the slender percentage of the firm's profits that Mr. Findlay allowed my father-in-law in deference to *his* father's memory. They had regarded me all the while as a catch! And indeed, from their point of view, I suppose I was one.

I should say at once that Pussy belonged to the first category of Mr. Findlay's "girls like that." She believed in what her par-

ents professed, not in what they did. There was not a worldly
bone in her body.

It is common today for young people to speak scathingly of
the former domination of American culture by WASPs, but, for
all their violence, they have little conception of just how dominating it was. In my youth American society and government
were almost entirely in the hands of big business and the legal
profession, and both of these were very white and very Protestant.
What we now call ethnic groups, Jews, Irish and Italians, had
managed to get hold of political organizations in the larger cities,
but even there the financial districts — the real centers of power
— remained predominantly WASP. I do not mean that there was
not plenty of opportunity in New York City for a young lawyer
of Italian-American origin, but if he wanted to join the Union
Club or the Piping Rock, if he wanted to send his sons to Groton
or Andover, if he hoped ever to be president of the American
Bar Association or achieve high federal office, it was going to be
a lot easier for him if he became an Episcopalian and treated his
homeland as an exotic memory rather than a present-day
inspiration.

Yet it would be totally to misinterpret Mario Fabbri to assume
that I adopted a religion and a social philosophy — indeed, a
whole new code of life — for self-advancement only. As a boy
I associated the Catholic Church and my family's Italian tradi-
tions with the rigors of an ancient class system of which we had
been the victims. I *believed* in the American way: in its deity, its
ideals, its good manners, its restraints, its orderliness and its clean-
liness. I still do. Of course, I perceive its faults — what child of
Italian parentage would not? — its priggishness, its prejudices, its
materialism, its hypocrisy. But it still seems a lot better to me than
what my parents ran away from. The tragedy of American
civilization is that it has swept away WASP morality and put
nothing in its place. Franklin Roosevelt was not a traitor to his

class, as his old college classmates maintained: he was its last great representative.

When Pussy and I were married in 1915 I was not yet a partner in the firm, but I was headed for it. Mr. Findlay accorded me the signal honor of attending my bachelors' dinner and even had several more than his usually moderate quota of drinks. When I asked him confidentially if he did not recant of his proffered warning, he simply shrugged and said: "Well, you picked a fine girl. Pussy has none of her father's weakness. We can be frank, my boy, you and I. But what she will never appreciate is your success, or why you care about it. I told you how it was, Mario. They go either one way or the other. And I don't know which is worse."

It was not long before I discovered what the old man meant. Pussy was the dearest little thing you can imagine, with brown eyes and chestnut hair and a kind of breathless enthusiasm, and she had seemed to find it terribly exciting that I was Italian and Catholic. I had been aware that she had a deep puritan streak and an exaggerated sense of civic duty — she spent half her evenings at a settlement house teaching poetry to telephone operators — but I had never doubted, despite my boss's warning, that I would be able to change all that. Once married to me, would not Pussy be glad to shed her girlish fads and share my tastes and enthusiasms? Should I not open up to her a larger life?

Never was fatuous man more deluded. What I had not gleaned — what man of Mediterranean background could have? — was that once married to me, Pussy should have conceived that I had become incorporated into the tight box of her own gray puritan fate. Oh, she loved me, yes, but she loved me now as a fellow prisoner, as one who had volunteered to leave his privileged seat in the arena and leap down to join her amid the hungry lions. The sacrifice was touching, no doubt, even overwhelming, but for better or worse I was now subject to *her* god.

By which I do not mean an Episcopalian god. Far from it. Pussy, like many religiously inclined Protestant agnostics of her generation, cared nothing for sect or dogma. Her god refused to be tied down; he was too busy tormenting consciences. Pussy was even shocked at my giving up Catholicism. She said it might look as if I were doing it for social reasons.

"Do you mean I can't give up something I don't believe in because someone might call me a toady?"

"I don't know," she murmured doubtfully. "Is that what I mean? Perhaps it is."

Let me hasten to add that, for all our differences, Pussy and I were basically happy. Not that she ever changed. Oh, no! The big income that I ultimately earned, the ostentatious way of life that I adopted (a Georgian town house in the East Sixties and a country estate on the north shore of Long Island), the private schools to which I sent our son and daughter, even my art collection of Post-Impressionists and Fauves — all of these she accepted without in any way altering the basic pattern of a daily existence largely devoted to school and hospital work. She never sneered at my enthusiasms; she rarely even criticized them, but she sometimes looked askance. She lived like an unimpressed poor relative in the midst of my glory. She was always perfectly amiable, if slightly *distraite,* as my hostess at dinner parties where the guests, wines and menus were chosen by me. I think that without my considerable contributions to her charities, she might have absented herself from some of these. But her puritan conscience would not allow her to accept something for nothing. Oh, yes, she was always just.

And she was the stronger of us two. That showed in the children. Both Alma and Tomaso were essentially hers. They were obedient and respectful to me, at least until they went to college and became tinged with radicalism, and I think they cared for me, in their own way, but Pussy was always the "real" parent.

Her murky god got his long fingers into their consciences, too, and made them view me somewhat in the light of a genial Philistine. Alma, fortunately, majored in the history of art and gave me substantial help with my art collection. It was thanks to her advice that I bought the Pisarro from the sale of which Pussy and I have largely subsisted since my disbarment.

Which ugly term brings me at last to Gridley Forrest. I had known him slightly ever since my marriage, for Mathilde, his wife, had been a classmate and cousin of Pussy's, but the two girls were too different to be congenial, and we had seen little of the Forrests until the late nineteen thirties, when he became a judge at the federal circuit court of appeals. It was he who then sought my company, he who initiated the friendship, if that is the proper word for the relationship that developed between us.

But a word first about his wife, Mathilde, which name she pronounced in the French way. She had been brought up in the same fashion as Pussy, but if ever there was an argument in favor of heredity over environment, it was the contrast supplied by these two. Mathilde, presumably, was the other type of New York girl to whom Mr. Findlay had so darkly referred. She was no more like my Pussy than if she had been born and raised in the Antipodes. To begin with, she was beautiful and blonde and had a bewitching charm of manner. And then, instead of suffering from Pussy's deep sense of personal unworthiness, Mathilde took for granted that every gift life tossed in her lap was not one jot more than her due. Indeed, as a girl she had considered that fortune had rather scanted her. Why had her family had to make do with a shabby brownstone house off Gramercy Park when the Vanderbilts had marble palaces?

Her marriage to Gridley Forrest, a young man of no particular means or social position at the time, had come as something of a surprise to her friends, but when they learned that he was not only brilliant but forceful, they decided that she knew what she was doing. His legal future seemed assured, and Mathilde certainly did not care whether money was old or new so long as she had it. When it later became apparent that Gridley had political and judicial ambitions, these were perfectly acceptable to her, so long as he had put aside enough to make up for any diminution in income.

Mathilde would never, beyond the merest civility, have much to do with any of her husband's legal or political associates who were not of her own social set. In this she actually regarded herself as morally justified. Once, when I ventured to suggest to her that it might help Gridley if she would broaden herself a bit, she retorted that, thank you very much, she was not going to turn herself into a hypocrite for the sake of money or high office! But I must admit that she was a delightful woman — when things were going her way. She was bright and observant and could be very funny. And she certainly played a marvelous game of bridge.

Much later I learned another of her characteristics. She was a tribal creature, and when society condemned her husband, she accepted the verdict without question. Yet I do not believe that she had the smallest sense of personal outrage at what Gridley had done. That was all some kind of senseless man's business. But when she heard the chief medicine man, so to speak, proclaim the outlawing of her husband, what could she do but join the others in the ritual dance? She was decent enough to Gridley when he came out of prison, for she had a basically kind nature, but she continued to dine out and to play bridge in houses where he could not accompany her. Perhaps it was just as well. Cooped up alone they might have come to loathe each other.

Gridley Forrest, I sometimes think, was put on this earth to destroy me, the one being equipped by a malign creator with the apparatus fatal to my defenses, as the mongoose is to the cobra or the desert wasp to the tarantula. That word *wasp* again!

He had an uncanny way of seeming to enter inside of one, to rummage around in one's basement or attic, turning up this or that, pulling soiled clothes out of baskets, and all with an air of total matter-of-factness, as if it were something he had to do, a kind of chore — perhaps, indeed, just such a thing as you would naturally do to him, if you only could.

He was a very large man, portly but square-shouldered and strongly built, with a shiny bald dome and a severe square face, small but pronounced features and gray, cold eyes that glittered with a seeming severity behind his pince-nez. He was always opulently and immaculately dressed, either in dark suits, or, in the country, in rather surprisingly loud tweeds. He was never loved by underlings. Yet he had an astonishing way of achieving rapid intimacy with people, once he had decided that he wished it. It was almost as if he might ask you, on a first acquaintance, if you had slept with your wife before you married her. And yet his manner was so direct, so judicial, that one hardly resented it. There was even something a bit flattering about it. You were raised to his level. You might even begin to wonder if he would not tell you if he had slept with *his*.

The Forrests and the Fabbris exchanged dinner invitations perhaps twice a year, but Gridley and I did not become personal friends until my election to the Greenvale Country Club in 1934. I should admit here that election to this club was the social triumph of my life. I never could see why Pussy and the children found it stuffy. I enjoyed it just as much as, during my two years on the waiting list, I had thought I should. I loved the big white shiny clubhouse, always so freshly painted, with its porticos overlooking the great green stretch of the golf course merging in the distance with the green or golden woods; the huge sapphire swimming pool; the grass courts; the smart women in tennis clothes with well-set golden hair and golden jewelry. My son, Tom, said that I liked it because it looked like a Packard advertisement. But wasn't a Packard advertisement meant to convey the idea of a luxurious and agreeable existence?

Forrest played golf every weekend at the club, and soon after my election he started asking me to join him. In the course of a year this became an established thing. We met every Saturday to play eighteen holes and have a couple of drinks afterwards in the bar that looked over the riding ring. Forrest never asked anyone to join us, and he was not a man whom one approached without a bidding, even in that club. I don't think he was ever much interested in people. An audience of one was all that he needed to discuss his two favorite topics: the craft of judging and the state of the real-estate market, in which he had invested Mathilde's money and his own savings. Of course, I was more interested in the former, but with a couple of large construction companies among my clients, I cared a good deal about the latter as well. Forrest would always indulge my curiosity with fascinating tidbits about his cases and fellow judges before pumping me about housing developments. I was perfectly aware that I was being pumped, but I had no objection. Was I not, in my own way, pumping him? It was useful, in my practice, to know all I could about his court.

He knew that I admired him as a judge, and he took my admiration, like everything else, for granted. He had a just rather than a conceited view of his own distinction, and he fitted himself appropriately, I thought, into the history of the American judiciary. Only he was less sanguine about his future than I. He shook his head with sudden, sharp irritation when I once predicted his ultimate elevation to the Supreme Court.

"Not a prayer!" he retorted. "I'd have as much chance as John W. Davis, and he's Roosevelt's *bête noire*."

"But Davis is an arch-conservative. Even if he is a Democrat. You haven't opposed the New Deal. Is there a single piece of FDR's legislation that you've held unconstitutional?"

"No. But a man's got to be more than neutral these days. He's got to be committed, dedicated."

"Well, you weren't even against the Court-packing bill!"

"That's true, too. Roosevelt was right about the Court — with four judges committed to the theory that the Fourteenth Amendment was designed to protect the big corporations! But he still should have waited. Time gave him all he wanted."

"But how could he have known that?"

"He should have taken the chance. What had he to lose? The NRA and AAA hadn't worked, anyway. The Court saved him the embarrassment of having to scrap them. But that's where Roosevelt showed his smallness. He was vindictive. He wanted to get those old men. He wanted to rub their noses in his Court bill. And he never forgets a slight. Count on it, Mario! From now on every justice appointed to that Court is going to have to be a man who will make old MacReynolds and Butler vomit all over their black robes!"

The image seemed unduly violent. "You mean a radical?"

"It's not so much who it will be as who it won't. And it *won't* be a man who can make any kind of judicious assessment of the balance of power among the three branches of government. It won't, for example, be Gridley Forrest."

"Roosevelt isn't going to be in office forever."

"Don't bet on that! We're living in a revolution. It's going to be a long time before moderate men are listened to."

"I hate to think that."

"Then think *this*," Forrest said grimly. "In any other period of American history, with the possible exception of the decade immediately preceding the Civil War, I could have looked forward with some confidence to ending my career as one of those nine men. Not now. And yet some deluded folk think I've had a successful life. Why, I've been the unluckiest man of my era!"

It was rare that our talks struck so emotional a note. Gridley

Forrest was not often given to dramatics. Even when the day came that he offered me a front-row seat to the greatest of dramas. You'd never have guessed it from his tone.

It was on a Saturday at noon, after our usual round of golf, over our usual whiskey. As I think back, perhaps he *was* a bit graver than usual. I had been talking about my score, a record for me, when he suddenly interrupted.

"I assume, because you are involved in patent law, that you have read the decision in McFarley against Baker Thermos?"

"Oh, yes. A surprisingly good opinion. For Judge Freer."

"You agreed with it?"

"I did. Although the question was certainly a close one. It must have been a happy day for the thermos company."

"Very happy. An adverse decision would have bankrupted them."

"I didn't know old Freer was so expert in patent law. Did you assign him to the case?"

Forrest's stare now became almost hypnotizing. "I did," he replied in a rather gravelly tone. "And I even gave him some assistance in the opinion."

What was I supposed to say to *that?*

"That surprises you?" he continued.

"Until you have explained it."

"Preston Saunders is president of Baker Thermos. He paid me — shall we call it a retainer? — to assure the decision. I gave Freer twenty percent of it."

What do you feel when you are face to face with history? A curious numbness. I saw a picture with Forrest in it, and with myself in it. I was a person quite apart from myself. I heard a voice droning somewhere behind me. The voice seemed to be telling me that this was the greatest judicial crime in the history of the United States. But it wasn't real, or if it was real, it was something flat and ordinary. There was not, it seemed to me, so much difference between fact and fiction, or even, for that matter, between crime and innocence. There was simply the judge and I, and our golf game, and now his sale of justice. His simple, matter-of-fact sale of justice.

"You are speechless. It isn't surprising. You see a desperate man before you, Mario. Everything I have is tied up in real estate. I had to do what I did to avoid foreclosure on the key parcel. I saved myself in the nick of time." As I simply continued to stare at his impassive countenance, he went on in a brisker tone: "You wonder why I am telling you. Because the case is on appeal. To *my* court, of course. And Saunders couldn't keep his mouth shut. What corporate executive can? He blabbed to one of his VPs. And now that VP has sent me word that if they lose the appeal, he will expose me. So there you are, Mario. If the decision in the district court is not affirmed, you will see me prosecuted, convicted, imprisoned and forever disgraced. My name will become a symbol of infamy in the history of American law."

How could a man take it that way? How could he sit there, surrounded by all the showiest trappings of an American success story, and so resolutely face his own annihilation? For a moment the little girl on her pony preparing to take a jump in the ring beneath us was blurred. Then I saw her again. She was on the other side of the jump. She had cleared it nicely. I recalled somebody's theory that no moment of time is ever lost, that they are all recorded somewhere, in an infinite library of tapes. Surely this moment would endure as long as any.

"You are still speechless. Do you think I am pulling your leg? Or do you think I have taken leave of my senses?"

"No, no. I believe you. You couldn't joke about such a thing."

"Good. Then, to the point. Will you help me? If not for my own sake, for the reputation of the bench?"

I gazed at him in surprise. Then I nodded. "For *your* sake, Gridley."

His answering look betrayed nothing. He might or might not have been touched by my personal concern and affection. But I suspected that he took these things, like everything else, for granted. Which did not mean that he did not value them. "Very well. I accept your kindness. Indeed, I must. I have discussed the case with Judge Tobey. He is adamant for reversal. He considers himself an expert on patents. That leaves Judge Isaacson. I think he might be persuaded. But I shall need to show him a draft of my proposed opinion affirming the decision of the lower court. It must be very persuasive. It can be written only by you."

* * *

I went to work immediately to write a legal memorandum, or what really amounted to a brief, that Forrest could offer Judge Isaacson, presumably as his own work or that of his law clerk, to persuade him to sustain the opinion of the lower court. I knew that the argument would have to be short and to the point; it would have to be in the form of a note, or series of notes, that Forrest might have dictated to his secretary in order to set down on paper the ideas that had occurred to him in reading the briefs of opposing counsel. In preparing my paper I was resolved to use no assistants, neither a junior partner nor an associate nor even my secretary. I would not so much as ask the librarian to bring me a reporter: I was determined to get all the books for myself.

"No, Mrs. Millis, I want to see if I know where everything in the library is," I told that loyal but bewildered lady. "The trouble with us older partners is that we get too dependent on helping hands. And I'm going to work right here at this table, if you don't mind."

"But can't I get Miss Stairs to take down your notes, sir?"

"And bother everyone in the library with my dictation? Certainly not. I shall write out my own notes like anyone else."

Some of the younger partners, alerted to the senior's "mysterious research," came in to offer to help me, and I had to try my darndest not to betray my irritation.

"We have really come to a pretty pass," I could not help retorting testily to one of these, "when the presence of an older partner in the library, reading a Supreme Court opinion, is news that rings from one end of the office to the other!"

What I was doing was attempting to encapsulate my crime, so that nobody else would be in the smallest degree contaminated. I take no great credit for this; it seems to me that it was only elementary decency. But I never believed that I was doing a thing that was morally wrong; indeed, I believed that it was morally right. Which does not mean that I was under any illusion as to how my conduct would appear against the canons of legal ethics. I knew that I was engaged in assisting a bought judge to persuade an innocent fellow judge to sustain a bought decision. I did not even try to persuade myself that it made any difference that the brief I was writing might have been submitted with perfect propriety by counsel for the litigant for whom I was indirectly working, or that I was not being paid for my efforts. I knew that, even had I been the innocent counsel of the bribing appellee, my clear duty on learning of the hanky-panky in the tribunal below would have been to alert the appellate court. Disbarment would be the inevitable and deserved result of my being caught.

Yet I was actually exhilarated! I was strangely clear in my mind and heart that I was not only justified but praiseworthy in my act of judicial subornation. I say "strangely," not because I have changed my opinion today, but because, in view of all the horror that ensued, it does seem curious that I should not have had more doubts. I think I may have felt some still unsettled debt to the great nation that had rescued my family from the sad poverty of its origin. I had believed in the American system, in hard work, in getting ahead, in a society that at least tried to be fair to the individual if that individual had only some respect for it. I had prospered in that society, and now there was something I could do to show my gratitude.

A cover-up, the listener will shriek. How could anyone feel that way about a cover-up? But remember that the term has been given a particularly foul name by Watergate. Who knows how many of the heroes and inspiring events of our history do not owe some of their luster to cover-ups? Are we absolutely sure that secret tapes in the White House would not have told us some very disturbing things about Thomas Jefferson and Abraham Lincoln? And be frank now, you who hear this tape. Supposing — just supposing — it had been possible to cover up the Watergate break-in and spare the world a knowledge that has disillusioned millions with the very concept of democratic government. Would you not have done so?

The basic moral question is whether or not he who covers up believes, with any basis of reason, that the criminal will not repeat his crime. I believed, certainly, that Forrest had taken only one bribe and that he would never take another. And I accepted — and still accept — the principle that the concealer of a crime must be condemned, legally and perhaps even morally (though the latter may seem illogical), if his attempt fails. His is a lonely decision. He has taken the law into his own hands. He must not complain if he is caught. He has elected to be his own judge and jury. He has sentenced himself.

But I refuse to hang my head; that's the point. Even today.

Pussy, who always seemed indifferent to my enthusiasms, was extremely sensitive to my anxiety.

"You're worried about something," she said, when I was having a double whiskey before dinner on the day that I had delivered my handwritten memorandum to Forrest. "Has it anything to do with Gridley Forrest?"

I could not help staring at her as if she were a witch. "Now what on earth gave you that idea?"

"I had lunch with Mathilde today."

"You did? I thought you never lunched with her."

"Well, she joined me at the club. She wanted to talk to me. She's afraid that Gridley's having some kind of a nervous breakdown. Very moody and can't sleep at night. Drinks more than usual." Here Pussy glanced at my dark glass. "She thought he might have told you something about it."

"When?"

"In one of your golf games."

"We haven't played in two months. Perhaps he's worried about his work. It can be a heavy burden to be a judge."

"It would be for me, I'm sure. But for Gridley? I should have thought he was the perfect Solomon. Utterly cold and detached."

"Perhaps he's worried about Mathilde's bills. She lives very grandly for the wife of a federal judge."

"Well, that's his fault. He should put her on a budget."

"I didn't say it wasn't his fault," I retorted testily. "I was attempting to explain his anxiety."

Pussy considered this for a moment. "Yes. It would be hateful to be married to Mathilde if you couldn't give her everything she wanted."

"You've never really liked Mathilde, have you?"

"Oh, 'liked.'" Pussy shrugged. "Does one really like or dislike childhood friends? It's a special relationship."

It was not long after this that rumors began to circulate in the downtown bar that Judge Forrest was on the take. The first one that I heard was from one of my partners at lunch. It was Tom Tray, a younger man, very serious, a dedicated lawyer for whose rise in the firm I had been directly responsible.

"I know you're a friend of Judge Forrest's," he told me gravely. "That's why I wanted to be sure you know what people are saying. No matter how unfounded it may be."

"They're saying he sells his decisions?"

"They are."

"How can people be so irresponsible?"

But Tom did not even shake his head. "They say his wife's a reckless spender. Isn't it the oldest story in the world?"

"But a circuit judge, Tom!"

Tom gave me what I thought was a rather queer look. "I guess they're not all angels."

A week later the story broke. Gridley Forrest was indicted for bribery. The news ran in mammoth headlines. In that less sophisticated era when, to quote the disillusioned Macbeth, we were "but young in deed," the public outrage reached a pitch almost inconceivable today. We had not seen both a President and a Vice-President resign from office under fire. But my personal dismay may be imagined when I read in the newspapers that the United States attorney had selected as the basis for his prosecution *only two* cases of Forrest's alleged sale of decisions. And these, according to general rumor, were but the tip of the iceberg! Forrest had apparently been seeking money wherever he could find it. To shore up his collapsing little empire of stores and warehouses in Queens and Brooklyn he had been desperately bartering justice to the first comer, receiving every kind of shady middleman in his very chambers, talking unguardedly on a tapped telephone, even committing himself to signed memoranda!

But my dismay was equaled only by my consternation on the morning when I faced the indicted judge himself seated before my desk. Gridley Forrest was actually asking me to represent him! He was as grave and impassive as if he were having a drink at the Greenvale Club after one of our golf games. None of the tenseness of which Pussy had spoken was visible now.

"Of course you're pleading guilty," I managed to articulate.

"Guilty? Certainly not. I deny the whole ridiculous business."

"But, Gridley! You *know* what I know!"

"Never mind what you know or don't know. It will be your job to see that the U.S. attorney proves his case. *If* he can. There is no end of hurdles that can be set up. Hearsay, privilege, malicious intent to defame a judge, even entrapment."

"You mean you're really going to fight this?"

"To the end!"

For several moments I sought words in the angry red tumult of my mind. Then I gave up. "Not with me, Judge."

"You mean you decline to represent me?"

"Absolutely."

Oh, that gray metallic stare of his! It was the last time I ever saw it. Or him.

"You'll let down a friend in need? Take care, Fabbri. The friend in need may let *you* down."

I rose. "Good day, Judge."

* * *

Unlike my former friend, I did not fight my accusers. When the Bar Association, acting on the evidence introduced in the trial by Forrest's attorney of my participation in the patent case, instituted disbarment proceedings against me, I was permitted to resign as an attorney in the state of New York upon admission of the charges. Although I was not technically disbarred, my disgrace was complete. I have been able to make only a small living since as a real-estate broker. But for the sale of my art collection I should at times have suffered actual need.

The hardest part of the whole business was my family. Pussy greeted my misfortune as an early Christian might have greeted the chance to detach a centurion from a Roman legion and lead him with her to the glory of martyrdom. Her nobility in disaster was almost unendurable. The only thing that kept me from leaving her was that she left me. She was so horrified when I told her that I felt no repentance that she moved for a time to her old mother's. But when she came back, it was to accept me, brazen and unrepentant as I was. We managed to remain on civil terms until her death two years ago.

Tom took the drastic step of changing his name. I believe that he did this to show that he was not afraid of incurring the odium of deserting a parent in trouble. It takes guts for a gentleman to look like a cad, but Tom had those guts. He detested my crime and deplored my intransigence; he saw no alternative but to cut himself off from me forever. I simply hope that he has not regretted it. If he has, he has shown no signs of it. He is a successful physician and has a large family that I have never seen. God bless him.

Alma accepted me and my crime. It was happy for me that in marrying she was able to shed my name without a moral problem. Her children are almost cozy with me; they think I was a "victim of my time," whatever that means. Alma has a comfortable theory that I was confused between an Italian Catholic upbringing and something she calls "the Protestant ethic." Between them, anyway, I am considered virtually without blame, a dear old wop grandpa who is not to be taken quite seriously.

There is a young man today, however, who is writing a Ph.D. thesis for Columbia on the implications of the Forrest case. He has been to see me several times, and I have come to like him. He has a theory that Gridley Forrest was subconsciously trying to destroy the judicial system of the United States in revenge for not having been appointed a justice of the Supreme Court. He was delighted when I supplied him with the confirming evidence of Gridley's hatred of FDR. I do not know if I believe in his theory, but it certainly gives a dignity to my saga which is preferable to Mathilde's shopping bills.

Charade

$\mathcal{M}$ADGE DYETT FELT that the year 1937, which had marked for so many of her friends a turning point in the Great Depression, seemed only to confirm its permanent doom for herself and her parents. They continued to live in the shabby, four-story, red brick house on East Thirty-fourth Street, but only because they could not sell it, and the top floor was rented to an uncle and aunt. Her father was out of work and prattled all day, with a self-confidence that nothing could justify, of his financial prospects and plans. Madge had had to give up college and take a job teaching at Miss Fairfax's School, of which she and her mother were alumnae. Her only future seemed to be to stay there until she was old enough to retire.

She had a vision of herself that was jarred every time she caught her reflection in an unanticipated glass. When she was prepared for the vision — gazing affectionately into her bedroom mirror, carefully turned from the garish sunlight, a long tress of brown hair pushed artfully across her high forehead, the small, full, pink lips half-open and a brooding expression in her grave brown eyes — she could at least try to see herself as an emancipated young woman of the years immediately following the war, some poetess or social worker of 1922, wasp-waisted, plainly dressed, earnest, idealistic. But the figure that she saw suddenly thrust at herself in the long mirror of a hotel lobby, even if thin and trim enough, suggested nervousness and fatigue. Nor was there any question that the left cheek on that long, perhaps lugubrious face bore two pockmarks. Oh, yes, she was angular! Hers was not a body that men lusted after. What else was a body for?

She sometimes felt that it was only her parents' attitude that made her life so intolerable. Through the years, without ever explicitly recognizing her father's failure, her mother had seemed to admit it in her abandonment of all outward manifestations of success. Elaine Dyett had let her weight increase until she could only be called dumpy, and her once pretty features had been largely lost in puffed, powdered cheeks and a double chin. She got dressed later and later in the morning, and her billowing wrapper, spotted from meals on trays, from chewed candy, from surreptitious sips from bottles, came to be Madge's mental image of the home. Yet innate fairness made Madge admit that her mother was never querulous or self-pitying; she seemed, on the contrary, oddly content with her solitary sybaritism. Elaine liked to keep up with the gossip of the great world, even though that world had passed her by; all the diversion that she appeared to need was to cut away, with complacent little snips, at the reputations of old friends and acquaintances who had acquired any degree of fame or fortune. Her conversation had reduced itself to a mild, continuous little stream of disparagement.

Had Madge been impressed by Mrs. Sabatière, the fashionable mother of one of her pupils at Miss Fairfax's School? "Mrs. Sabatière? Muriel? Oh, don't give me Muriel Sabatière." It was Elaine's illusion that people in the great world were constantly being "given" to her. "She was born Muriel Barclay, you know. Of the Barclay Street Barclays, yes, but a poor branch. I remember her at school: six feet in her stockings, with hair as straight as nails. Where did I read that some crazy portrait painter had boasted how he had caught the 'elf' in her? Elf, my hat! Her parents were happy enough to snag Paul Sabatière, though how they caught even him, I've never known. The gossip had it that old Tom Barclay had to get down his shotgun. And now Sabatière has dressed her up like a French doll and piled his collection of jade and porcelains around her and made her one of the sights of the town! But I'm afraid I'll always think of her as the gawky schoolgirl who peed in her pants in assembly. And I suppose nobody remembers now that her husband was blackballed at the Union Club because of that business with old Mrs. Carey's trust?"

Madge had long been indifferent to her mother's interpretations of a world that they saw through different glasses, not because Elaine's readings were inaccurate — there was always a grounding of truth in them — but because they were no longer relevant. Her mother might not want to be "given" Eleanor Roosevelt, but Eleanor Roosevelt was still First Lady of the land. There was something unseemly to Madge in this constant dredging up of ignoble aspects of the past, particularly when she contrasted it with the habit in all the Dyetts of dressing up their own failures in robes as grand as those they stripped off the real winners. The combination of praise of self and denigration of others, both false by all current values, made a world of stifling fantasy.

But 1937, as it turned out, was to bring a great change in Madge's life. Thanks to the illness of an older teacher, she was asked to take over the English class of the twelfth grade, girls who would be coming out at debutante parties in the following year, or traveling around the world, or learning languages in European pensions, or even, in a few instances, going to college. Only four years before Madge had had some such dreams herself! Now she was only a plain brown figure, associated in the bright young heads before her, she bitterly assumed, with boring textbooks soon to be cast aside.

It needed no great experience to spot Lila Sabatière as the

leader of the class. She had all the qualities admired by students and deplored by faculty. She was dark, striking, pretty, vivacious, mean of tongue and yawningly bored by everything but clothes and men. She managed to seem chic even in the ugly uniforms required by Miss Fairfax: round green bloomers with flat-heeled shoes and black stockings, and on Fridays, when, to every teacher's dismay, the girls were allowed to wear what they wanted, she would saunter in, looking like a page from *Vogue.* She was dreaded by the older teachers for her ability to make fools of them by questions seemingly naive but actually designed to bring out a salacious interpretation of a passage in the text which the innocent pedagogue had missed. Madge was determined that the girl should not make a fool of *her,* and she kept a wary eye on the whispering corner where Lila sat with her small coterie of intimates.

"I think you had better sit up here in the front row, Lila, where we all can hear you. It seems a pity that the others should miss your witty comments."

So Madge started her first class in English 12, and so she was resolved to keep it. But for some reason, probably because the girl was playing a deeper game, there seemed to be little trouble as the weeks progressed. Lila sat with pencil poised, her eyes fixed on the teacher, as if she were actually engrossed in what Madge was saying about Shakespearean tragedy. On the day when they had the trouble about *Hamlet,* it seemed almost more Madge's fault than Lila's. Apprehension may have made the former too tense. The topic set for class discussion was the comparison of Ophelia's madness with that of the prince.

"Of course, we have no reason to doubt the genuineness of the insanity in Ophelia's case," Madge led off. "But we may not agree as to its cause. Is it really grief over her father's death? Or is it the fact that Hamlet was the killer? Or does she see in Hamlet's violence a further rejection of herself?"

Lila's hand was in the air. "I suggest, Miss Dyett, that Ophelia went mad because she was so continually insulted."

"That's interesting, Lila. How was she insulted?"

"Well, every time another character lays an eye on her, he tells her not to go to bed with Hamlet. Laertes talks about her 'chaste treasure' and Hamlet's 'unmastered importunity.' Her father prates about the dangers of pregnancy. And Hamlet tells her that her only hope is to get herself to a nunnery. Obviously, they all think she's a complete tramp."

Madge suspected that the girl's language was a challenge to herself, but she was still impressed by her perceptions. "You must remember, though, that in Elizabethan drama a great emphasis was placed on virginity. It is not only Ophelia but *all* the heroines who are constantly being warned."

Lila glanced about the room. "Like us."

A general laugh broke out, and Madge felt bleakly isolated. All these girls had a "chaste treasure" to guard from aggressive males, while she . . . "Let us return to Hamlet, please!"

"It's just that things haven't changed that much," Lila continued boldly. "I guess we all know what it's like to live in a world where men want you to be virtuous and loose at the same time."

"Lila, that will do!"

"Small wonder Ophelia sang dirty songs when she went off her nut. What else had men taught her?"

"I said, that will do!"

"Oh, come now, Miss Dyett, you're not *that* much older than the rest of us."

"Lila Sabatière, will you please leave the room!"

Later that morning, when Madge was sitting alone in the tiny office that she shared with two other teachers, on the top floor of the converted brownstone that housed the school, she looked up to see Lila standing in the doorway, still unabashed.

"If you think I owe you an apology, I apologize, Miss Dyett. But I meant well. I only thought you were one of us. You're so much younger and brighter than the other teachers."

It was elementary, Madge knew, that a teacher should never succumb to flattery, but she simply collapsed.

"It doesn't matter," she muttered, flushing. "I was feeling a bit tense this morning. I have a ghastly headache."

"I shouldn't wonder, with a class like ours! I'm sure in your position I'd be fit for a sanatarium. But perhaps, then, this isn't the moment to ask what I was going to ask."

"About Ophelia?"

"Bless you, no! Ophelia can take care of herself. Or could have, if she'd ever learned to swim. No, I was wondering if you would consider taking on the job of tutoring me at home. Mummie said it wouldn't hurt to ask you. She'll make it worth your while."

"Tutor you in what?"

"All the things I'm going to need for college. I'm horribly behind in everything."

"I didn't know you wanted to go to college."

"I didn't. But it's a changing world, and I guess I'd better change along with it. A debutante isn't the glamorous creature she used to be."

Madge couldn't help smiling. "I'm sure *you* will be, anyway, my dear."

"Well, of course, I can go to college and still come out. But, seriously, would you consider the job?"

And so it was, the following afternoon, that Madge found herself outside the Sabatières' house on Sixty-seventh Street. Such houses, or mansions as she liked to call them, she knew only by their facades, but from the East Fifties to the East Nineties she knew them all. She had little interest in their architectural merit; it satisfied her that their total function, as Veblen might have put it, was to proclaim the wealth of their proprietors. For this purpose it did not matter how crudely they were Gothic or French Renaissance or Greek Revival or Minoan, and Madge even liked one extravaganza on Fifth Avenue that rose from a French door sheltered by a marquise to an attic modeled on the Porch of the Maidens. She knew that she would recognize Number 34 when she saw it, but she could not remember it by its number alone, and she was delighted when it turned out to be one of her favorites: the purple Jacobean manor house with the two large bay windows on the *piano nobile*. She had no patience with those who maintained that such a facade should have overlooked a wide green park with peacocks or a lake with swans. She was quite content to have it in town.

The interior to which the impassive butler who answered her ring ushered her was dark with a sense of expensive things gleaming and glinting. She followed him swiftly up the low-stepped stone stairway, across a wide landing, and past a huge hunting tapestry to the gleam of an elaborate Louis XVI parlor, where a tall woman rose to greet her from behind a tea table littered with silver.

Madge had never seen anyone quite like her. Muriel Sabatière was arrayed ("dressed" would have been too common a term) in a sumptuous, ankle-length gown of crimson velvet, heavily interwoven with gold braid, and she wore a choker of rubies. She was large, with broad shoulders, but she was also slender and held herself very straight. The initial impression of fortitude was softened by the extreme femininity, even the affectation, of her airs and graces. Her large gray eyes flickered; her laugh was tinkling, almost intentionally artificial. The "haunting beauty" of which Madge had read in the society columns was made up in part of fine but very regular features in a long face and in part by the tricky makeup of the extended eyebrows and pink lips and by the elaborate frizz of small curls into which her auburn hair exploded at the back and sides of her head.

When Madge's new employer had reseated herself to preside over the tea tray, her arms seemed to flow like the necks of the swans that did not swim outside.

"Why do you think my little girl wants to go to college, Miss Dyett?"

"She says it's the modern thing."

"And so, no doubt, it is. But why should she want to do the modern thing?"

"Young people are very conformist, I find."

"It occurs to me, Miss Dyett, that as Lila's mind seems to harp on the opposite sex, our clue may be there. Is it possible that the young men today are more attracted to industrious college girls than to idle debutantes?"

"I don't suppose they have to be too industrious."

"Happily for darling Lila! I think I knew your mother, Miss Dyett. Wasn't she Elaine Strong?"

Madge assented, reflecting on the social distance indicated by her mother's vivid recall and Muriel's vague one. Indeed, why should anyone remember Elaine?

"Well, let us accept the good consequences," Muriel said blandly, returning to the subject of her daughter, "regardless of the motive underlying them. I am glad, anyway, that Lila wishes to learn and that you will be teaching her. I have no doubt that we can all profit from you. I want you to feel a member of the family. There! I am going to start right off by calling you Madge. And I want you to be a friend of my son, Barclay, as well."

"He's a little boy?"

"No, my dear. He's a very big boy! He goes to Columbia Law School. I hope your presence at our table may induce him to take more of his meals at home."

Her smile was radiant, stylized, artificial, and yet ... *Could* it be sincere? Mrs. Sabatière was an actress, a would-be Bernhardt, so stagey that Madge almost had to laugh. The tall woman looked beyond her visitor, as if to an auditorium; she seemed to scan upper balconies as she clasped her hands; she almost curt-sied. It was a perfect curtain call. But what was it all about? Why should she want the tutor to be a friend of her son's? Or was it all just frou-frou?

So, anyway, Madge's new life began. Muriel Sabatière proved exacting; she required the tutor to come to the house three nights out of seven and to spend weekends at the country place in West-chester, but as she paid generously and as Madge had nothing in the world that she would rather do than watch the Sabatières in their own setting, Madge was perfectly satisfied.

Lila's brother, Barclay, at first sight seemed as handsome and romantic as Madge could have wished, and her heart leaped at the prospect of the fantasies that she could embroider around his image. Were not his raven locks and shining eyes precisely what her scenario required? A Byronic hero? He had better manners, too, than any such, for he took the trouble, at Madge's first din-ner with the family, to be affable to her.

"They tell me Lila's the very worst student in the whole history of the school," he said, making a face at his sister. "And Miss Fairfax remembers back even to Mummie's day!"

Madge wondered if he should have been quite so jokey; the Corsair would not have deigned to notice a kid sister. She ob-served now that his cheeks, instead of being pale and long, were round and almost ruddy, and that he had a habit of taking a small comb from his pocket and slipping it quickly through his hair. Barclay was nervous, and not like a panther but a domestic cat. He wriggled too much and giggled too much; he was always looking warily about as if to be sure that nobody was laughing at him. And he was patently terrified of his father, jumping up in an exaggerated military, almost heel-clicking, manner when the latter came into the room. Barclay seemed to relax only with the women of his family.

His father was a man who could turn his charm on and off like an electric light. It was as if he were hoarding what he regarded as a dangerously limited quantity; the moment it was not needed he would resume his habitual impassive stare and gruff manner. And then, when he wished to please again, the fiery little gleam in his opaque green eyes, the rumbling chuckle and liquidly articulated compliments were reactivated. There was a truculent independence in Paul Sabatière that seemed to make it difficult for him to sustain a flattering attitude even with the most important persons.

His bald, gleaming dome and quasi-military stance gave him a definite air of distinction; yet there was nothing, so far as Madge had been able to make out, of the aristocrat in his background. He was reputed to be the bastard son of a French priest who had arrived from nowhere and made a fortune, no one knew quite how. A poor Barclay had been the best Paul could find for a wife, yet he had perceived, with the eye of a maestro, just what could be done with her and how she could be trained to be the striking centerpiece of his collections. He had supervised everything personally: her hair, her makeup, her clothes; he had coached her in elocution and gestures, all with the idea of making her not the most beautiful or the most accomplished or even the most charming woman of the New York social scene — none of these would have been possible — but simply exotic. The danger had always been that people might laugh, but if they didn't — and it was his genius to predict that in the long run they wouldn't — what could they do but stare? And ultimately admire?

Muriel, Paul and Barclay were, of course, new to Madge, but she found that Lila was, too. The girl was as much of a capitalist as her father; basically she respected only those whom she had not yet bought. The moment Sabatière coins, however few of them, jangled in the tutor's thin purse, the tutor belonged to her. Lila continued to treat Madge cordially, but she was much more casual now; the relationship between pupil and teacher had become more like that between mistress and lady's maid. Madge found that they did their work at Lila's time and place and no more of it than Lila strictly cared to do. But why should she object to this? Obviously, Lila's college career, if indeed she should bother to have one, was going to be a minor episode in a life devoted to quite other things. If she chose to gossip during their study period, where was the harm? Only when Lila once directed that they should meet after school at the Dyetts' house instead of her own, and then never showed up, did Madge object. The next morning at school she took her too-independent pupil aside.

"I can't be used as a cover for dates that your mother doesn't know about."

"Oh Madge, how can you be so stuffy? I thought you were going to be such a *friend!* All we did was go to a lousy movie."

"Well, you might at least have told me."

"I will, dear, I will. Next time."

"There's not going to be a next time."

"And I was thinking of asking Mummie to let you take me to Europe!"

It was a bribe that pulverized Madge. She knew that Lila had no immediate plans to go to Europe, but as Madge had never been abroad and wanted to go more than anything in life, she dared not take the smallest risk.

"If your mother finds out, it won't be just a question of my job with *her*. It'll be a question of my job at the school!"

"Trust me, dear!"

Madge didn't trust her, not for a minute, but she decided that she had better pretend to. The Sabatières had become all the family she wanted to have.

The "home" on Sixty-seventh Street thus adopted by Madge
was easily extended to include the country seat of the Sabatières
in Westchester, a greenish-gray François I *hôtel* which seemed
to miss an urban environment as much as the town house missed
a rural one. But Madge missed nothing; she felt her soul stretching itself out, like Browning's "long cramped scroll," to freshen
and flutter in the breeze of this new life.

It surprised her that she should always find herself seated by
Barclay at the family board. When the party was only five, this
was almost inevitable, but when, as was more usual, there were
guests, it seemed to show a design, and certainly not Barclay's.
But why should his parents behave in precisely the opposite way
to what might have been expected of them? Why should they
encourage the proximity to their only son and principal heir of a
plain, impecunious female?

Barclay himself seemed sufficiently at ease with her, but it was
the same jokey, faintly evasive ease that he showed with his
mother and sister. He liked to tell her mildly off-color stories,
and she had a sense that at all times he had a supply of stronger
ones waiting in the wings, so to speak, for her smallest encouragement. This was never forthcoming.

"Why don't you take Miss Dyett to the horse show this afternoon, Barclay?" his father demanded one Saturday at breakfast.
"She might like to see the jumping."

"I thought I'd better study, sir."

"Study? On Saturday afternoon? Isn't that a bit stiff?"

Barclay flushed, with the resentful-but-obedient-little-boy look
that he adopted for this somehow menacing parent. "You're the
one who wishes me to get good grades, sir."

"Oh, very well, go to your books. But if I catch you roaming
about the place the way you're apt to do when you say you're
working, I shall consider that you have used Miss Dyett very
badly."

"Can't she go with Lila?"

"With Lila!" Mr. Sabatière sneered. "This young lady wants a *man*. Damn it all, when I was a young buck, I didn't moon over books on a lovely spring day when there were ladies about!"

Barclay looked more sullen than ever. When he rose to leave, he bowed stiffly, even a bit absurdly. "If you will permit me to say so, sir, nobody obliged *you* to study law."

Madge, embarrassed by this interchange, turned to Lila when they were alone at the table and asked why Lila's parents seemed to be pushing her at Barclay.

"They think Barclay's terrified of women," Lila replied with a shrug. "They must be hoping you'll break him in."

"Do I really look *that* type?"

"Is there a type? My old man has a dirty Gallic mind. He thinks he can get what he wants by yoking you and Barclay together."

"What a charming image! I don't feel very complimented."

"Well, I wouldn't take it too seriously. Parents are always up to something idiotic. So long as Daddy doesn't take it into his head to set Barclay an example, you have nothing to worry about."

"Set him an example?"

But Lila was already bored with the subject. Barclay did not interest her. "Let's put it this way. Daddy's not very good at keeping his hands to himself. Half the girls I ask home complain about it."

* * *

Muriel Sabatière remained as she had started, a stage presence. She had no conversation, only monologues.

"I remember your mother at school quite well, my dear. She and I were the products of a stricter day. Oh, my, yes! We were almost Chinese in our reverence for the past. Old New York — dear, dim, quaint, brownstone old New York! It had values, I fear, that we have largely lost."

Madge was to be reminded forcibly, on the very night of this soliloquy, of the decline of manners in her day. She was also reminded of Lila's warning. After Lila and Muriel had gone upstairs, she had lingered by the fire to listen to Mr. Sabatière playing the Moonlight Sonata. He played it heavily and he made mistakes, but there was feeling in his rendition. When he had finished, she thanked him.

"You like music, Miss Dyett?"

"I like it when it's played as well as that."

"Dear me, your ear must be very untrained." He came over to her chair and suddenly reached out a hand to cup her chin and raise her face to his. "You know, my dear, you're really prettier than you think you are."

Madge was conscious primarily of admiring her own poise. She gazed boldly back at him as Joan Crawford might have done in a movie about a shopgirl with an amorous boss. "What makes you think I don't regard myself as irresistible?"

He chuckled, half-scornfully. Then he leaned down and kissed her on the lips. His were large and soft; they felt like rubber. And his breath was bad. He straightened up.

"Would you like me to do that again, Miss Dyett?"

"No, Mr. Sabatière, I shouldn't."

He raised his eyebrows. "You believe in skipping the preliminaries?"

She caught her breath at his presumption. But then she reflected that she had received his kiss. To such a man this was the equivalent of a complete surrender, and if not, *tant pis*. What did he care? And what would he do for her? Give her a jade necklace in return for one night? Madge's nose wrinkled as she associated the odor of his stale breath with the odor of her parents' bathroom, whose door seemed always to be left open.

"That kiss was a preliminary to nothing, Mr. Sabatière."

"Very well. I see you're a sensible girl." He chuckled. "That little pass was only a test. I like to be sure of the virtue of any friend of my daughter's — *and* of my son's." He lowered one eye in a half-wink to show that he was only half-serious, as he turned to the stairway. "Turn out the lights, will you please, when you go up?"

Alone, Madge reflected bitterly that he had not even bothered to ask her not to tell his wife. He didn't care if she did!

It was late spring now and very warm. The next morning Madge rose early. She liked to walk about the place before it became too hot. She could more easily indulge in fantasies that she was its chatelaine when there was no human presence about, other than an occasional gardener, equally taking advantage of the cool in order to get his work done more comfortably. She roamed in the gardens, although flowers bored her; she looked at the statues of mythological subjects, although they were as bad as most garden statuary; she visited the stables, although horses alarmed her. She admitted to herself that a country estate had little value to her except, as in her favorite Veblen phrase, to demonstrate "conspicuous consumption." But there were times, and this was one, when her mind became weary of the very persistence of her fantasies. If she *had* been Muriel Sabatière, what would she have fantasized herself as being? A queen? An empress?

As the heat began to steal over her, she became aware of a headache, one of those that would increase rather than diminish as the day wore on, and she sat down in the shade of the Spanish patio by the swimming pool. She chose a seat close to the wall, not to be unobserved by anyone who should use the pool but simply because it offered the most protection. But she was suddenly frozen to a tense stillness as she recognized that she must indeed be invisible to the person she was now beholding.

Barclay had walked out of the pool house and was standing by the edge of the water, stark naked. This in itself was not so surprising. A man alone at that early hour would not wish to be bothered with bathing trunks. And Madge was not ignorant of the male nude; she had been to art class. His well-shaped if pale and slightly puffy body had no surprises for her — but one. His male organ was erect. As she stared in astonishment he seemed to be looking right at her, with a fatuous little smile. And then he twitched his hips.

But he was *not* looking at her. He was looking at a figure that she now observed crouching in the flower bed at the far side of the pool. It was one of the gardeners, a man of middle years, bronzed and brawny, with a long, rather equine countenance. He had put down his trowel and was staring back at Barclay. Madge could make out in his Italian features a frank interest — the interest that any sexual question would at once arouse in him — an amused disgust, and greed.

He rose and strode slowly down the length of the pool to stand close to Barclay. Then he suddenly grabbed him in the groin and pulled him into the pool house.

Madge found herself almost running back to the big house. Slowing to a walk, she tried to make sense out of her own jumbled reactions. Why should she be shaking all over? Had she been aroused by Barclay's state? Disappointed that she was not the cause of it? Disillusioned by this evidence that she was never likely to be? For if Barclay were to give up gardeners, it would surely have to be for a woman more alluring than herself. "No," she cried angrily aloud, stopping to stamp her foot. It was none of these things. It was simply one more proof, if proof were needed, of how little use the world had for her!

"Very well, Madge Dyett," she exclaimed, "you're on your own. As if you hadn't always known it!"

But she was on her own with a new asset; that was the point that she brooded over all that day. After breakfast, at which she darkly watched a rather febrilely chattering Barclay, she spent much of the morning in her room, putting together the pieces of the puzzle that he had left her. How long, to begin with, had he been indulging in these practices? Undoubtedly for some time, for the boldness of his self-exposure to a family employee hardly implied a virginal venture. How dared he take the risk? Precisely because the thrill lay in the risk! Madge had read enough of psychology in college to know that the dangers of blackmail and of betrayal to a parent of whose wrath he lived in constant dread might have given poor Barclay half his pleasure. And then to perform those acts under the very nose of the august sire — wasn't that just a son's revenge? Wasn't there an exact precedent in Proust's chapter where Vinteuil's daughter and another woman make love before the composer's portrait?

Surely she wished Barclay no harm, but the time had come to use him. If her suddenly conceived project should work, it would redound as much to his benefit as to her own. Courage, Madge Dyett!

The Sabatières gave a dinner party for twenty that night, and she found herself, as usual, next to Barclay. The dining room was paneled in Chinese lacquer: dragons and tigers prowled in forests; exotic birds took wing high over blue lakes toward snowy peaks. The huge porcelain centerpiece represented the rescue of Orion from his foundering craft by dolphins. It was a bit difficult to see all one's fellow guests across the table, and the high-backed red Venetian chairs were set sufficiently apart that one had to speak distinctly to be sure of being heard by one's neighbor. This, however, was what Madge was counting on; once two heads had approached, there was a privacy rare at dinner parties. And it was impossible for Barclay to run away.

She fixed the pitch of her voice so that it would just carry to him. "Why do you never trust me, Barclay?"

He was startled. "When do I not?"

"You never tell me anything about yourself. Anything personal, that is. You're always making jokes. You're never serious."

"What do you want me to be serious about?"

"Oh, anything that you really care about. Your love life, for example. You can't tell me a man as handsome as you doesn't have a love life."

His relieved smile readily granted this; oh, he could talk as long as she wanted in this bantering mood! "But men don't tell those things to girls. Not to attractive girls, anyway. What sort of a fellow would I be if I boasted to you of my conquests?"

"I'm not an attractive girl, Barclay. And if I were, would it make that much difference to you?"

His eyes glittered. "What makes you say that?"

"Simply that I have a notion that attractive girls don't interest you very much. Not at this particular stage of your life, anyway."

He caught his breath. "You mean because I have to work so hard?"

"That's it," she replied flatly. "Because you have to work so hard." She paused to watch his gathering reassurance. Then, abruptly, she changed her tone. "Barclay, I repeat, why can't you trust me? I only want to be your friend. Not the sort your father wants me to be. A real friend, with no nonsense about sex. I know *I* need one, and I strongly suspect you do."

"Why do you think I need a friend?"

"Do I have to tell you?"

"Yes!"

"Very well. For the same reason it would do me no good to make love to you."

Oh, he was staring now! "And what is that?"

"What happened at the pool this morning."

For a moment she feared that he *would* bolt.

"You've been spying on me!" he hissed.

"I have not been spying on you. I happened to be there, and I couldn't help seeing what I saw. Never fear. I wasn't shocked.

That sort of thing strikes me as perfectly natural. I wouldn't dream of telling anyone." She paused again to let him consider these assurances. When there seemed no further danger of his leaving the table, she went on: "Let me put something else to you. I shall keep my voice very calm and matter-of-fact, and you must try to do the same. All right?"

He seemed almost hypnotized. "All right."

"If you have many friends like this morning's, you must get blackmailed from time to time."

"Friends?" He was still not entirely subdued. "What makes you think there's been more than one?"

"Oh, Barclay. What do you take me for?"

The remnants of his morale now collapsed. "All right, yes, I've been blackmailed." His voice took on something of a whine. "You can't imagine what my life's been like, Madge. I've got to believe you don't want to make it worse."

"What I must convince you of is that I want to make it better. What would you say to a life where you could give up the law, travel, see the world, sail, dance, ski — anything you fancy — and at the same time enjoy complete sexual freedom with the complete approval of your family?"

"What would I say to that? I'd say you were describing paradise! But why play games?"

"This is no game. It's yours for the asking."

"Asking what?"

"Asking me to marry you. Now wait!" She reached over to touch his wrist in a quick gesture of reassurance. "There wouldn't be any sex in it. The marriage would be a mask. The mask of a deep friendship and mutual understanding. We would be partners. Partners against the world!"

He was interested — oh, yes, he was intensely interested! "You mean I could do anything I wanted, and you could —"

"Do anything I wanted," she finished for him. "Only I don't

think I'd want to do so much. If I could just get away from my family and my job and do some traveling — well, that would be paradise enough for me."

"But I begin to see it!" he exclaimed, with rapidly rising excitement. "Mummie and the old man would be so tickled to see me married, it should be duck soup to talk them into my quitting law school. And then why not a year's honeymoon? Why not a trip around the world? Think of it, Madge! Samoa, Tahiti, Ceylon, Naples, Algiers. Oh, my God! A whole year. And after that? Well, who cares what happens after a year? Madge, you're a blooming genius!"

She now had her first moment of misgiving. She had a sudden vision of a long series of hotel suites where she would sit alone while Barclay pursued beautiful brown young men down golden beaches. Then she became aware of the patiently waiting old gentleman on her other side.

"We have to turn," she murmured to Barclay. "That's enough for now."

It was not, however, to be enough for long. Later that evening, in the drawing room, when after their brandy and cigars the gentlemen joined the ladies, Barclay, ignoring his mother's frantically signaled instruction that he sit by her guest of honor, came over to rejoin Madge. It was obvious that he had had several brandies.

"Your mother wants you to sit with Mrs. Stiles," she warned him.

"To hell with Mummie! I've been bored enough already listening to the men curse out Roosevelt and talk smut. I've been thinking over our plan. And do you know what? The more I think of it, the greater it seems! Why don't we get married right away? Next week?" He laughed aloud at her look of dismay. "Well, next month, then?"

* * *

What was most surprising to Madge about the announcement of the engagement, simultaneously in the *New York Times* and the *Herald Tribune,* was how quickly it was accepted by everyone as a perfectly natural thing. The elevation of a humble teacher to the glittering rank of the Sabatières, after the first flurry of surprise, was rapidly assigned to the order of normalcy. "After all, who *was* Paul Sabatière?" her aunts were asking already, to the irritation of her mother, who had now decided to upgrade her daughter's new in-laws.

Muriel had been delighted from the first. She had folded Madge in silken arms with an air of total acceptance that would have been difficult even for her to feign.

"Oh, my dear, this is just what I have dreamed of! A lovely, sound, sensible and sensitive girl for my too volatile boy! Darling, you'll be the making of him! Oh, what things we shall see! His father has been a bit put out by his wanting to leave law school, but I tell him it will be only a leave of absence. And a trip around the world is just what you both need, at just this moment! Ah, my two darlings!"

Paul Sabatière had gruffly assured Madge that all Barclay really needed was the shaping and finishing influence of a clever woman.

"In my day," he told her candidly, "that would have been the job of a married woman in society, some years his senior. But other times, other ways. I am satisfied that you are a very accomplished and sophisticated young woman. He should flourish under your care."

Paul even condescended to take her father out to lunch and listen to the latter's ridiculous stock-market theories, while Muriel called on Elaine and behaved as if nothing had interrupted their school intimacy of thirty years before. Miss Fairfax herself was quoted as saying that the match was "all in the family."

Barclay, somewhat to Madge's irritation, appeared to adore

the whole thing. He was almost hilarious at the little parties that followed the announcement, and he was elaborately polite to everybody, except when he would drag her off into a corner, like a too amorous fiancé, and explode in fits of private laughter.

"Oh, Madge, has there ever been a couple like us before? Is there anything you and I couldn't pull off together? I declare, I shall end up falling in love with you."

"Maybe I'd better get a page-boy bob."

"Darling, your *tone*." And then he simply roared again with laughter.

Once Barclay had accepted the idea of a confidant, he embraced it with the same fervor that he must have formerly reserved for his hidden sex life. But Madge soon discovered that she was paying a price for the easy success of her stratagem in the unending flow of his confessions. Barclay's repressed sexual history exploded before her in syrupy waves. There seemed no end to it. She was appalled at how early it had all started; there was no detail of grapplings in boarding-school cubicles, of rendezvous in the woods at summer camps, and, later, of elevator boys, grooms, taxi drivers and sailors that she was spared. He told her not only of the affairs he had had but of those he had wanted to have, or even dreamed about. His longings and his accomplishments were of equal importance to an imagination that seemed always on fire. And never once did he probe into her private life; she existed to be an ear, never a tongue. One night, sitting up late at the nightclub La Rue, she at last ventured a protest.

"You never ask me about *my* life!"

"But you told me you didn't have any," he protested, with some justification.

"Well, you might ask if I'd ever wanted one."

"But tell me! Talk, dear girl, please talk! Isn't that what we're here for?"

And, of course, she couldn't. What fun would it be to make up a tale of frustration?

Lila's attitude had been distinctly different from that of her parents. She had been casual, faintly sarcastic, about Madge's advent as a sister-in-law. The tutor had moved up several pegs in the eyes of the world, but Lila seemed to want it known that she was not of those who were impressed. There was even, in her oblique glances, a note of something like conspiracy, and Madge finally determined to have it out with her.

Lila could never resist a shopping trip, and she accompanied Madge on some of the rounds for the purchase of her trousseau. At a department store, as they passed the maternity counter, Madge indulged a perverse impulse to pluck the girl by the elbow and murmur: "Don't you think, if Barclay and I are going to be abroad so long, I should stock up here?"

Lila smirked. "You do keep it up, don't you?"

"Keep what up?"

"Look, honey. This is Lila. Remember?"

Madge stared. "Remember what?"

"Who do you think you're trying to kid?"

"I hadn't been under the impression that I was trying to kid anybody."

"Except people who don't happen to know what your marriage to poor old Barclay is all about!"

"Lila Sabatière, are you implying something about your brother?"

"Nothing *you* don't know, dearie." But as Madge continued simply to stare blankly at her, Lila continued, shrugging: "Only that he's . . . well." Revoltingly, she linked her thumbs and made her fingers flutter to simulate the wings of a butterfly. Madge felt a belt of dampness tight around her heart.

"And do your parents think that, too?"

"*Think* it! Darling, they weren't born yesterday. Daddy, after all, is an old frog, and Mummie, for all her fey airs, was brought up on a farm in Rhinebeck. She knows what cows do to each other!"

Madge felt suddenly sick. Her mind seemed to turn over and reel. "And they suppose I'm the sort of girl to cope with that?"

"Well, darling, *aren't* you? Honey, it's a compliment! Have I upset you terribly?"

"Not at all. It was foolish of me to worry about being the user, when I've been so comically used."

"Oh, dear me, now you *are* mad. And everything was so perfect! Mummie said you were everything in the world she had dreamed of for Barclay!"

"How long has she known about him?"

"Everyone's always known about Barclay! Everyone but Barclay himself. For some reason he's always thought he was getting away with it."

Madge nodded sadly. "It's a common illusion. I should have seen it. Oh, what a fool I've been, Lila! But just what did your family expect me to accomplish?"

"They expect you to convert him, of course. Madge, where are you going?"

But Madge did not answer; she did not turn back or even wave. Fifteen minutes later, still in her hat and coat, she confronted Muriel Sabatière, seated behind the tea table, as when Madge had first met her. Barclay's mother seemed to be expecting her; she held up a piece of sugar with the sugar tongs and smiled radiantly. But she was not wearing the ruby choker, as she had on that first day. After the largest stone had been removed to be set in Madge's engagement ring, the string had been too short to go around even that slender neck.

"I was just hoping somebody would drop in for tea. How delightful!"

Madge remained standing. "Mrs. Sabatière, you knew about Barclay!"

"What did I know about Barclay? Not too much, I'm afraid. Oh, mothers, mothers!"

"You knew about the other men."

"I warn you, darling. I shan't listen to a word against my boy!" But there was no trace of indignation in that tone. It might have been some kind of lofty joke.

"I don't want to say anything about him. I only want you to tell him our engagement is off."

"Shouldn't that sad piece of news come from you, dear?"

"If he cared, yes. But he doesn't care. Ours was a business arrangement, pure and simple."

"Can that not be binding, too?"

"If I married him and left him, I might be tempted to ask for a settlement. This way everything will be cleaner and cheaper. And more honorable."

Muriel at this seemed to react for the first time. There was almost a throb in her voice. "Ah, my dear, stay with us! You are strong. You will change him."

"And how do you propose that I manage that?"

"A woman can do anything with a man. If she wants to enough."

"The way you did?"

Muriel hesitated. Then she nodded with a suddenly brisk assurance. "Very well. Yes. The way I did."

Madge, desperate, became almost brutal. "By dressing up?"

Muriel's stare might have concealed anything. "Yes! By dressing up!"

Madge, closing her eyes, had a vision of the gorgeous tapestry that the willpower of this woman held over her family. For a moment she was almost tempted to emulate her. To defy chaos with the robes woven by a simple faith in one's own power to weave! But then it was as if she heard an imagined cough behind that imagined arras. Who could be concealed there but a pinching old man with bad breath? And who was the real weaver?

Deliberately now she removed the ruby ring from her finger and came forward to place it on the silver tea tray. "I'm sorry, Mrs. Sabatière. If there was anything I could do for you, I'd gladly do it. But there isn't. At least now you can wear that wonderful choker again!"

Sketches of the
Nineteen Seventies

The Mendicant

---

*H*E HAD ALWAYS BEEN a conscientious member of the boards of charitable organizations. He had contributed to them, modestly, like other professional men, lawyers and doctors, good people, solid people, with roots in the city stretching back a hundred years or more. But who, in a day of foundations and corporate givers, cared for the widow's mite?

When the children's hospital of which he was president was threatened with insolvency, he resolved to save it. He and his wife dressed up and went out. They joined the glittering world of the charity ball. They dined with the rich; they spent their vacations on yachts. They visited in Palm Beach, in Fishers Island, in Southampton. They were loved for their warm hearts and manners. He saved the hospital. Hundreds of children were benefited.

One night I sat by him with the men at brandy after a large and splendid dinner. I was surprised at how loudly he laughed at the vapid jokes of our red and stertorous host, who had drunk too much. Yet his amusement did not seem in the least affected. Those tears of merriment struck me as genuine. Only when he dried his eyes, still heaving convulsively, did I catch a glimpse, behind his silk handkerchief, of a gray iris as hard as agate.

Grief in Jet

HEN ALBERTA'S HUSBAND DIED, at only fifty, of heart disease, she felt depleted. Relief was only in numbness. At moments it seemed to her that she must have died herself. Two days after the funeral her sporty, octogenarian mother, whose doctor had forbidden her to come north for the services, telephoned from Palm Beach.

"A girl's place is with her ma at a time like this. Come on down, love."

"But, Mother, you've always got so many people around!"

"You won't see a soul. Honest Injun."

Alberta flew down and found the old lady an unexpected source of sympathy. For two whole days they sat on the patio or strolled in the garden. They sipped iced drinks and ate cool, clever meals and talked with restful familiarity. Alberta's mother was wise, crisp, funny, sensible. Alberta began almost to believe in a future again.

On the third morning, when she came down to breakfast, she found her mother arranging place cards on a table set for a lunch party of twenty-four.

"Why do you look at me like that, Alberta? Do you mean to mourn all your life?"

The Acoustiguide

THE TOURISTS CAME IN, each with a small talking box tightly clasped to one ear. They seemed for a moment to hover, veering slightly to the left, then to the right, like a flock of geese reconnoitering a pond, and then, with a final concerted flurry of decision, they descended to form a tight round huddle before the Mona Lisa. There they hung in mute attention while a voice instructed them about dates and prices and thieves. The little lecture over, they rose again from the waters of contemplation, without so much as a glance at the glorious Leonardos on either side of the smiling one, and flapped off honking to the Winged Victory of Samothrace.

Euthanasia

---

*W*HEN DEATH FINALLY CAME to the bedside of Eric's ancient father to perform his tardy office, Eric, outraged at what his family had been put through, caught him by the elbow as he was leaving.

"Look here, Death. You're way behind the times. You ought to catch up. As we learn new ways to lengthen life, you should be learning new ways to kill. Who wants to sit mindlessly blinking in a wheelchair? Who wants to be a burden on his children? And the expense! Do you realize the old are now blowing their life savings waiting for you? That they have to be damn near millionaires to afford the usual terminal ailment? Speed up, damn it all!"

Death nodded. "You're right, Eric. But there's only one thing I can do for you. Come with me now."

"Now?"

"I'm much faster with men your age."

Eric drew back.

"I guess I'll take my chances. After all, if worse comes to worst, I can always swallow a pill."

Death laughed as he took his leave.

"If I only had a dollar for every time I've heard that one!" he exclaimed.

Old Age in Orbit

ALFRED HAD ALWAYS SAID that he looked forward to retiring from the bank at sixty-five. At last he would have time to do the things he really wanted. He could take the chairmanship of the hospital drive. He could enroll in courses at the New School for Social Research. He could paint. He could garden. There was even that history of the bank he had long yearned to write. And he would get to know his grandchildren better. He would teach Timmy to sail.

He had reckoned without Mabel and the tyranny of climate.

"But in the spring we have to go to Greece. It's the only time. Well, we can have either snow in Zermatt or sun in Antigua. What's the point of sitting home in slush?"

Behind her, like the growing multitude of brooms in *The Sorcerer's Apprentice,* he saw the rows of affluent, bronzed, sexagenarian couples, waving their ski poles, their putters, their tennis rackets, dressed by Abercrombie & Fitch, calling to him to join them in sport, in travel, in life.

Alfred now hires an accountant to do his income-tax returns. His former secretary sends out his and Mabel's Christmas cards, and the letters to the children have degenerated into long-distance calls. He promised us this year to work a week on the hospital drive, but he sent a check instead, from Tunis.

The Blue Grotto

*I*N THE HUDDLED DARK I feared that I should strike my head against an overhanging rock. Dozens of little boats rammed their way past each other, crammed with laughing, squealing folk. An American wag shouted a deafening "O Sole Mio." It was like a temple of love at Coney Island, a house of laughs, a fun palace. Only when I happened to look back did I see, in the light from the entrance, the sparkling, sapphire, translucent water where Axel Munthe and the emperor Tiberius had swum.

Easter on Fifth Avenue

*I*N THE EARLY YEARS of the century the Easter Parade marked the pedestrian return of the fashionable family from the mid-morning service, up or down Fifth Avenue. The furs, the pearls, the strutting, all emphasized the secularization of faith. But today we have gone one step further in the long march from the twelfth century and the Cult of the Virgin. The avenue is now closed for traffic on the holy day while thousands of suburbanites in shiny shoes and new bonnets, who have driven into the city for nothing but this purpose, jam the thoroughfare in thick, multitudinous throngs, strolling, eddying, swinging, pushing, neither looking nor looked upon, heirs of a social form distorted beyond recognition, of whose very origin they are ignorant, while television cameras from the roofs of trucks record the amazing phenomenon.

Henry Adams wrote that the Virgin looked down from her altar on an empty church and a dead faith. She did well not to go outdoors.

The College President

$\mathcal{H}$E CAME TO THE CLUB late for our small men's dinner, looking very tired. He revived a bit after sitting by the fire and sipping an opaline martini in a frosted glass. Then, safe behind the craggy walls that shut out the shouts and the slogans, he cleared his mind of the anger that he had had to control all day. Sharply, he deplored the strident voices, the smelly bodies, the chanted obscenities, the cheap cynicism. It was an obvious relief for him to be able to shed his daytime mask of iron and rub his weary face.

The next morning we read his statement in the *Times*. "The interrelationship between radicals and questioning students has been a positive, constructive phase of university development in America."

It is the ironical triumph of youth, in its impassioned war on hypocrisy, to have created a nation of Tartuffes.

Sic Transit

At the reception given by the chairman of the board to celebrate the promotion of the new executive vice-president, who was only thirty-three, many of the younger bank officers and their wives were present. Residents of White Plains, of Plandome, of Short Hills, they surveyed the splendid Park Avenue apartment of their host and studied the other members of their vast organization with eyes that missed nothing. The men were bright and clean and smart; the wives were bright and clean.

The great lady whose late husband and father-in-law had been presidents of the bank a dozen mergers back, serene in the confidence of her eighty years, her uncountable wealth and a name that occupied its own chapter in every history of Wall Street, moved slowly among the younger folk, bowing like a dowager queen, gracious in her sense of favors bestowed. They nodded back politely and asked each other in whispers who she was.

"Do You Know This Man?"

$\mathcal{A}$LEXANDER HUME WAS SO PLEASED with the beautiful phrases of his will that he almost looked forward to his own demise. His collection of seventeenth-century paintings and drawings was bequeathed to the Manhattan Art Institute, to be shown in a separate room known as the Alexander Hume Room. A million-dollar trust fund was to be put aside for art research; scholarships were to be set up for study in Europe. But his wise old lawyer, eminent in the bar, persuaded him to keep his scheme elastic. "No man can foretell the future. The dead hand should not lie too heavy on the shoulders of tomorrow. Make your conditions precatory only. Trust to the discretion of your chosen beneficiary."

A year after Hume's death the art institute submitted his will to its counsel, who gave it a most gratifying construction. The obligation, if any, was moral only. The paintings were then sold, all except the Zurbarán, which was hung in the director's office, redubbed the Alexander Hume Room and so engraved on a small movable plaque which could also serve as an ashtray. The million-dollar fund was earmarked for curators' salaries, and the scholarships were converted into staff sabbaticals. Everybody at the institute was very grateful to Mr. Hume.

Some years later his portrait by an artist no longer fashionable turned up in a cleaning-out of the institute's cellar. Nobody recognized the subject, but a conscientious trustee, suspecting that it might be a former benefactor, insisted that the portrait be reproduced in the members' bulletin under the caption "Do you know this man?"

The Old Bachelor

SCHUYLER LANE WAS NOT in the least apologetic about being so long a bachelor. When I suggested to him that it looked as if he and I were going to be the last leaves on the tree, he reproached me with these words of wisdom: "I don't worry about that at all. Let fools rush in. I have no intention of making a final choice while the girl and I are callow creatures, blinded by the violent sexuality of youth. Less permanent relations will do me quite well for this period, thank you very much. When it comes to marriage, I have the highest standards! Mrs. Schuyler Lane will not only be beautiful; she will be accomplished in the arts and social graces. She will disgrace me neither in the hunting field nor in the drawing room. Money she need not have, nor lineage; I can provide both adequately. But she must be able to hold her own in any society in which we move!"

Schuyler was thirty-five when he and Amanda Cole became engaged. We were all eager to see what cynosure he had selected. And indeed, it seemed that she met all his standards. She was, it appeared, peerless, as affable as she was radiant, with no hint of snobbishness or superiority in her manners. She was nice to all of his friends, even to the least important like myself. No, we could not fault her.

They traveled abroad for the first year of their married life, and I did not see them until they came back, and I went to their apartment to call.

Amanda was sitting, rather inertly I thought, on the sofa; she said nothing to me, at least that I could hear. But I was struck by Schuyler's behavior to her. Never had I seen him demonstrate an attention so charming or an affection so touching to another human being. He explained to her any reference in our conversation that she might not at once comprehend; he joked about our "dull bachelor days" before his present "redemption." Love had not only touched his heart; it seemed to have given him one.

It was not till I rose to go and Amanda fell forward on her face that I realized she was dead drunk.

The Court

$\mathcal{W}$HEN MIDAS DIED, he bequeathed the whole vast fortune, so long coveted by his nephews and nieces, to a distant cousin, whose principal qualification, at least in his eyes, seemed to have been that she had never flattered him. But the bequest was welcomed by all but the disappointed. Magda, the lucky beneficiary, was a charming and intelligent woman, a trustee of cultural institutions and the popular hostess of a brilliant salon. People had always said of her what a pity it was she was not rich. Now a great new reign in the history of entertainment and philanthropy appeared at hand.

"I am going to be a very important person," she told me with the engaging confidence that was one of her charms. "Few people have ever come to this kind of wealth with my training and experience. The usual mistake that the very rich slip into is to allow a muddy little court to form between themselves and the outside world. But watch me! I shall make short shrift of flatterers and sycophants!"

And indeed it seemed for a time that she would. Magda gained the reputation of being able to spot oiliness and unctuousness under all the usual guises. She was universally praised for a crisp down-to-earthness that admirably set off her feminine charm. It was even said that Midas's greatest contribution to posterity had been to execute his will in her favor.

One night I dined at her house to celebrate another of her many honors, some gubernatorial or presidential citation. The company was brilliant, the wine and food of equal quality. It struck me, as I gazed about the glittering table, that we all shared the common denominator of a vital admiration for Magda. Toasts were offered; exhilaration prevailed. Yet I found myself at length uneasily aware of a new element in the picture. It struck me that that row of heads, turned toward Magda down each side of the table, might have been attached to a string that made them bob.

"Magda!" I cried in alarm. "Do you know something? We *are* a court, after all!"

Magda turned to me with a pale gape of astonishment. "But these are my dearest friends!" she protested vehemently. "They are all quite sincere!"

What she had said was perfectly true. But I had a vision of her head, too, now bobbing on that string.